BODY A

CW01465691

BODY AND BLOOD

BENYAMIN

Translated from the Malayalam by Swarup B.R.

HARPERPERENNIAL

An Imprint of HarperCollins *Publishers*

First published in English in India in 2020 by Harper Perennial
An imprint of HarperCollins *Publishers*

HarperCollins Publishers India, Cyber City, Building 10-A, Gurugram,
Haryana-122002, India
www.harpercollins.co.in

2 4 6 8 10 9 7 5 3 1

P-ISBN: 978-93-5357-811-4
E-ISBN: 978-93-5357-812-1

This is a work of fiction and all characters and incidents described in this
book are the product of the author's imagination. Any resemblance to actual
persons, living or dead, is entirely coincidental.

Benyamin asserts the moral right
to be identified as the author of this work.

Typeset in 11.5/15.7 Adobe Jenson Pro at
Manipal Technologies Limited, Manipal

Printed and bound at
MicroPrints India, New Delhi

HarperCollins Publishers, Macken House, 39/40 Mayor Street
Upper, Dublin 1, D01 C9W8, Ireland

To those who have fallen into the trap of trust.
And those who will.

Contents

Woe to you, teachers of the law and Pharisees, you hypocrites! You travel over land and sea to win a single convert, and when you have succeeded, you make them twice as much a child of hell as you are.

Bible, Matthew 23:15

PART ONE

Delhi

1

The WhatsApp message echoed like a cricket and landed on Sandhya's phone just as she was stepping out of the lift, filled with the pride of having posed an unusual question to herself – why were large mirrors installed on the three walls of the lift? – and of having answered it with sufficient gravitas, by deciding that no, it was not to shine one's face or pat one's hair into place, it was to ensure that one did not feel unsettled as one travelled alone towards the sky in this claustrophobic cell by creating a feeling that one had one's own reflection for company.

She flipped open her leather bag mid-stride and started searching for her mobile. This was such a curse. She always forgot into which pouch she'd hurriedly dropped the mobile. At times it would lie along with her lipstick, face cream, eyebrow pencil and comb in the pouch on the left side of her bag. Or in the small pouch in the middle, with her purse and the New Testament that she always carried with her which had 'The Gideons International Gift of Love' on the introductory page. Or with the sanitary pad and Chetan Bhagat's novel in the extreme right compartment. In spite of wanting to find a

permanent place for it every single day, she never could. Which
is why she kept missing many calls. And listened constantly to
complaints that she never answered calls.

She searched for her phone with the firm resolve that if
it was some message which spouted stupidity, she would just
delete it and exit from the group, even if it had people she was
fond of. This was another curse. That bloody message would
come only when she was in a tearing hurry to go somewhere.
And after searching frantically, thinking that it could be
something important, it would turn out to be terrible Sardarji
jokes heard ten thousand times before or God's own promoters
sending prayers to be forwarded to fifteen other people. And
then anger would surge through her. Many a time, she wanted
to hurl the phone as far as possible, wondering why, even in
this WhatsApp age, neither she nor God had any respite from
being attacked by these creatures.

Finally, by the time she managed to ferret the phone out,
Sandhya had reached the parking lot. 'Midhun had a small
accident. Come quickly to Medical Trust.' That was Rithu
Kurian's message. She faltered for a moment as though a black
bird had slapped her on the face. Then she tried calling Rithu
– but she was not reachable. She guessed Rithu might be in a
place where there was no signal – perhaps inside the hospital.

All through her scooty ride to Medical Trust, Sandhya
kept trying to console herself by thinking that there wouldn't
be any problem and that it would just be something minor.
She decided that WhatsApp had not evolved enough to
deliver any serious message. It never grew beyond kitchen

selfies, Sardarji jokes and small talk. If it had been anything serious, Rithu would definitely have called. Or sent an SMS. This was only a WhatsApp message. But just to be sure, at every red signal and at every major block, when the vehicle came to a standstill, she kept trying to reach Rithu.

Luckily, she got a call from Rithu before she reached the hospital. Rithu was waiting for her at the reception and took her to the ICU.

'The bike bumped into some vehicle and skidded on the highway. Some skin has been lost on the arms and legs. And there's a small wound on the head. The doctors said that there's nothing to worry about. He lay bleeding on the road for a while. That's all. The other vehicle sped away as usual, without stopping. Anyway, in which Indian city are bikers safe? They are the lower caste that anyone can hit and run.' Before they reached the ICU, Rithu Kurian briefed her about the situation in detail with a tinge of outrage.

Which was probably why Sandhya did not feel very scared when she saw Midhun through the glass window, strapped to monitoring devices and medicine tubes. Not only that, she believed implicitly that the God she trusted in would protect him and keep him safe under His wings, like He protected the dove from the eagle. In fact, it was this belief that had made her force Midhun into going with her to the prayer group meeting and then work on getting him to become a part of it.

2

It was when Rithu and Ragesh were planning to go to a movie straight from the office that Brother Aruldas called and informed her about Midhun's accident. They left for the hospital immediately. On the way, she WhatsApp-ed Sandhya the news. It was because she had no idea what exactly had happened and how serious things were that she chose to just WhatsApp. On reaching the hospital, she was glad that she had done so. If not, Sandhya would have really panicked.

By the time she reached the hospital, Dr John Samuel and Pastor Sam Philip were already there. And using their contacts and influence, they had ensured that Midhun got the best possible medical attention. Even in that moment of worry, Rithu felt a happiness tinged with pride about the fact that she had landed amidst people who spent most of their time for others. She could have ended up anywhere in this great big city. Even in dark alleys. But God must have decided that she should be with these people and, through them, find the path to goodness. Not just her, everyone in the group, including Ragesh.

Her only fear was that Sandhya would lose courage. But when she met Sandhya in that hospital corridor and told her what had happened, she realized that Sandhya had more courage than she thought. Not only that, Sandhya did not falter even as she stepped out of the ICU, wearing a hospital gown, after seeing Midhun during visiting hours. When Ragesh offered to stay the night as Midhun's caretaker, she turned him down affectionately and took it upon herself, almost as if it was her right. People imprisoned in their hostels and homes had to report faithfully every night. But there was no need for Sandhya, who lived alone in a studio apartment, to do this. Her space and time were hers alone. The intrinsic value of her freedom lay in the fact that she did not have to answer to anyone. And that was probably why nobody refuted her right to stay the night. They silently agreed that it was indeed Sandhya who should be beside Midhun that night.

It was based on the reassurance of Dr Samuel and the insistence of Sandhya that they – Rithu and Ragesh – left the hospital that evening, although a bit late.

But the next afternoon, a call from a totally bewildered Sandhya reached Rithu. And it was to say that Midhun's condition, which had been stable until then, had suddenly taken a turn for the worse, and that she was really scared.

'The doctors are not saying anything definite. The nurses said that there were a few complications. I have no clue what to do, Rithu,' wept Sandhya, who had lost all the courage she had had until then.

Rithu worked in an MNC that was based in Korea. One could not walk out of there with the same ease with which one could walk out of a local government office. It involved a complex process, with emails being sent giving detailed explanations and then waiting patiently for a reply to come in. But she managed to cross all these hurdles and reach the hospital in an hour.

'He was fine in the morning when I saw him, Rithu. We also spoke for a while...' she cried.

'The entire fellowship is praying for him. I am convinced that it will bear fruit. We were taught to believe firmly, without doubt. Then why are you so scared?' said Rithu, comforting her.

'Yes, that's the only way ahead,' said Sandhya. After a while, a dejected Dr Samuel walked out of the ICU and said, 'There was an internal haemorrhage that did not catch our attention yesterday. That has become worse. There have been many instances in my life when medical science was reduced to being a helpless spectator. Only God can lead our Midhun back to life. I know many lives that God gave back. Pray hard.'

Sandhya prayed. In all the languages that she knew.

3

The next day, Midhun's parents, along with two other relatives reached Delhi. Brother Aruldas and Pastor Philip picked them up from the airport. It was evident from the conversation on the way to the hospital that they were not aware of Midhun's actual condition. Though Pastor Philip tried to give them verbal clues, their minds were nowhere near considering such a possibility. They still innocently believed what Ragesh had said on the phone, 'No, there's nothing to worry – he just fell off the bike, that's all.' And that was what it was then. Something that was serious enough to be in the hospital for just two days. Whoever could have guessed that things would suddenly become worse?

Before they could see Midhun, Brother Aruldas took Midhun's parents into Dr Samuel's room. He had been instructed to do so in order to avoid a sudden shock. Dr Samuel gently explained Midhun's current condition to them. He advised them not to lose hope and to seek refuge in the God who performed miracles. His father became flustered. His mother started sobbing. The relatives who had come with them became restless. They refused to drink

11

the tea from the canteen. They just wanted to see Midhun. Dr Samuel himself took them to the ICU to see him. It was perhaps because he was too far gone that nobody strictly enforced all the stringent formalities that were part of entering the ICU. Everyone was just asked to wear a gown. A faint breath and the pulse of a few machines was all that was left of Midhun. His mother cried out loudly in vain to wake him. Midhun was unable to respond with even a tear. Brother Aruldas felt his heart ache. All of a sudden, he left everyone and walked out. This was the first time he was seeing Midhun after the day of the accident. Until now, he had only hung around with everyone else outside the ICU and kept asking Sandhya how Midhun was doing. But last night, more than anyone else, he was the one who had prayed for Midhun.

Sandhya was there when Aruldas came out of the ICU. She had moved away to the canteen for a while upon hearing that Midhun's parents were coming. Everyone said that it might be better to avoid meeting them at that point in time. There was a problem. His mother had been angry enough to call her a 'witch that traps young people between her legs' on the phone one day. Her friendship with Midhun was the reason.

4

It had been about six months since Midhun's mother had started accusing Sandhya, with and without reason. For everything that he did. For not picking up the phone, for not coming home for a while, for wandering around in the night, because someone saw him at a pub, for having bought a bike without telling anyone at home, for daring to put a picture of himself smoking on Facebook, for being online on WhatsApp for long hours after work, for having shifted house recently, for not having completed his post-graduation. Why, his mother kept blaming her for everything, which once made Sandhya sadly jest, 'Midhun, even if you go to the toilet twice a day, your mother will be upset and accuse me.' Yes, Sandhya was behind a few things that Midhun had done. But the truth was that she did not know many things either.

It was not like this before. They had entrusted Midhun to her as they would to a local guardian. They had not even met each other then. They kept hearing of a girl called Sandhya in their regular evening phone conversations with Midhun. They knew that it was this girl who had led their son – who had left home to do his PG in Delhi University, discontinued it halfway to do some computer programming and then moved on to do odd jobs that went on until the wee hours of the morning – to work for a fabulous salary at an MNC. When he started growing his hair long, when he started eating meat from dhabas, when he started blaming the harsh winter and started smoking, they knew that it was the same girl named Sandhya who called them up and said, 'He just does not listen to me Amma, you'll have to speak to him.' It was thus, without having met each other, that Midhun's mother and then his father became fond of Sandhya. And went on to believe that he would have the watchful eye of an elder sister on him in this unfamiliar city.

It was the same Sandhya who now moved away to the canteen to avoid meeting them. But after being away from the entrance to the ICU for a while, her heart skipped a beat and she decided that, no matter what they'd say, she needed to be as close to Midhun as possible.

She was relieved to see Brother Aruldas there when she came back. At least there was someone with whom she could share all the worrying questions that crowded her mind when she was alone. How can anyone who was really normal until morning suddenly take a turn for the worse? Can a small wound be so fatal? Has medical science not yet discovered a way to detect this in advance? Is there no medicine to bring such people back to life? Other than worries of his own, Brother Aruldas did not have an answer to any question. She felt that even Dr Samuel might not have the right answers. Sandhya concluded that medical science was only about possible attempts; no one could have implicit faith in it. Midhun's brain death that night proved just that.

5

Reality is a kind of darkness. We become quite disoriented when it envelopes us unexpectedly. And then the most important thing is the time we take to get used to that darkness and for the new vision to become clear from within it. This adjustment is critical for the process of coming back to life. This is the situation they were confronted by in Midhun's case. These were moments when they faced the reality that the person who had, until two days ago, laughed, played, biked, visited dhabas and joined them for prayer had suddenly gone behind the curtain of consciousness, into memory. Moments when they hoped deep within that no, nothing had happened – and even if it had, they could undo the last few minutes and bring him back to life. They lived under the sway of the tech world's 'undo'. When a tea cup falls from the table and breaks, when a paper document is torn unintentionally, when the bar of soap slips from your hand while bathing and falls into the commode, when you cross a red light that records your haste, when precious words accidentally slip out of your mouth, when children slip and fall and hurt themselves, this undo from the virtual world will pop into one's mind. Here, you have the opportunity to turn around, walk back into the past to repeat what you have done without making the same mistakes. The desire to do the same in real life often robs it of its seriousness.

They had to talk a lot to walk themselves out of that illusory dream. In reality, they were not walking out from, but slipping into the darkness. It was then that Sandhya fell on Rithu's shoulder and cried. It was then that Ragesh hugged Pastor Philip and sobbed uncontrollably. It was then that Dr Samuel tried to find solace in the enactment of the will of God. It was also then that Brother Aruldas stood staring at the sky like a frozen shadow.

But the two people who were sinking into the very depths of that darkness were Midhun's mother and father. Nobody could temper their sorrow with anything. The two relatives who had come along kept trying, but in vain.

Some people managed to move them to a room in the hospital. Brother Aruldas was assigned to be with them should they need any help. Friends dropped Sandhya at the apartment. Rithu stayed back with her. In the end, only Dr Samuel and Pastor Philip remained. In a short while, they were joined by Advocate Ram Manohar Varma. They had requested him to drop in. They met in the corridor outside the ICU that night to take certain crucial decisions regarding Midhun. There wasn't much talking. Just a few dispassionate gestures and decisions made with an acute economy of words. In the end, they entrusted Dr Samuel with the responsibility of talking to Midhun's parents to make them agree to release Midhun, who would never come back to life, to the eternal peace of life in heaven, and donate the organs that he would no longer need.

6

Midhun, we have no doubt whatsoever that you will want this. Which is why you had happily signed the form to donate your organs immediately after the awareness class organized by our group. And got the forms signed by your parents after fighting to convince them when you went home for the next holiday. And you, who idled on everything else, handed over the documents to Dr Samuel as soon as you came back and collected your donor card. And showed it proudly to Sandhya. And on that day, the day of the accident, you had kept the donor card safely in your wallet. Which is why we are convinced that you will be proud rather than sad that you are being donated in parts like this.

But will you ever understand the emotional conflict that we are going through to uphold your decision? It is far more painful to divide you among strangers than to accept the fact that you have left our friendship behind for the good fortune of eternal bliss. Though it sounds like a great thing, a great sacrifice, it is not easy to agree to it. If you were really and totally gone, the decision would have been easier. We would have no option before us. But Midhun, even though it's with the help of machines, life is still throbbing within you. We keep thinking that, somewhere deep down inside, you might still be listening to us stand and talk beside you, that you might feel our anxiety, our sorrow, and choke within, unable to react to anything. How then, can we agree, all of a sudden, to share you with strangers?

It was the day before yesterday, when we were coming back to the hospital, that Dr Samuel hinted at this for the first time, hinted that it was futile to wait for your return. That was the moment we fearfully accepted that you had surrendered entirely to fate. In the long silence and the emotional turmoil that ensued, each one of us slowly started moving towards giving our consent. We had no other path in front of us. Dr Samuel's scientific reasoning, Pastor Philip's spiritual reasoning and Advocate Ram Manohar Varma's social reasoning continued to brainwash each one of us. It might be more correct to say that, since they were important people in this city of ours and since we would need them again, we succumbed much faster. But Midhun, your parents did not need them. What did they have to think about other than you? Isn't it brutal to hope that they would accept your absence as quickly as we did? What cruelty. You might now stubbornly say that one should have the courage to face the intense light of life with one's eyes open, without being blinded by it. You've always said that. But Midhun, you will never understand the pain of losing a son until you become a father, until you become a mother.

Yet your father was brave. By evening, he agreed to release you for others. He promised Dr Samuel that he would get your mother to give her consent too. Based on that assurance, Dr Samuel reported the organ donation to the Medical Board. A team of experts arrived to certify that you were brain-dead, killing the last shred of hope we had. They drove the last nail into the coffin and wrote the report that you wanted.

7

Until the last moment, Midhun's mother hesitated to sign the consent form. She did not allow his father to do so either. 'Why this hurry? Can't we wait for a few more days? What if God gives him back to us?' she kept asking each one of us through her tears. But the recipients had already been found. All the arrangements to move Midhun to the operation theatre and to transport his life-saving organs had been made. The only technical hurdle to be crossed was the signature. Though everyone understood Midhun's mother and though everyone connected emotionally with her, there was no going back.

Finally, when Midhun's father signed the consent form, she passed out on Sandhya's shoulder thinking, 'You too have agreed to release him, you beast.' Sandhya and Rithu took her back to the room. By then, a few distant relatives and acquaintances who had heard the news had arrived at the hospital and they joined them in the room. It was doubtful whether Midhun knew any of them. They did not remember Midhun going to meet any of them in the last three years he had been in this city. Outside this group, he hardly knew anyone. Most often, his days began and ended with Sandhya.

It was his father who, with trembling hands, turned off the life-support system. And then closed Midhun's eyes. He was moved immediately to the operation theatre. In the next one hour, different ambulances sped to different hospitals in the city, carrying Midhun's organs. The story of that great donation was published in detail by different newspapers. Eyes for Manisha from Bihar. Liver for Harinder Singh from Punjab. Pancreas for Sukhdev from Patna. Lungs for Abdul Aziz from Kashmir. Kidneys for Ananthakumar Rao from Karnataka. Heart for the business tycoon Sundar Ramaswamy from Chennai. Through six different people, their Midhun would continue to live on.

Midhun, who always had a smile lurking on his face as though he had kept a naughty joke to himself, was taken back home on the evening flight. Along with his parents and the two relatives who had accompanied them, Brother Aruldas and Ragesh too were on the same flight. The expenses were borne by the Trinity Foundation.

PART TWO | *Goa*

8

Ragesh went straight to Chennai after Midhun's funeral. And then he sent an email to the office requesting leave. 'I will simply quit if they don't sanction it,' he said lightly to his friends. Midhun's death haunted him. He knew that he needed to go stay with his mother for at least ten days in the house in Nungambakkam, eat uthappam and curd rice made by her, and immerse himself in her love to ease, at least slightly, the pain that he was feeling. He said the same thing to Rithu when she called. 'You too should go home for a while. We will never be able to erase his memory. It will be good to stay away for a few days, though. Say what you like, at times it's a relief to be in your own home.'

Rithu also applied for leave the next day. The project manager, who was livid on seeing it, called her into his cabin, asked her what had happened and offered to set up a counselling session courtesy the management. 'I don't need counselling – what I need is a break from this madness,' Rithu said in a tough voice. He then started using frivolous logic. Spoke of four months of annual leave left. Reminded her about the pending work that had accumulated. Lamented the shortage of staff that the office was facing. Yet she stuck to her demand for leave for three weeks. She somehow managed to convince him that, if she continued to work in the situation she was in, her output would be affected. In the end, saying, 'Rithu, only because it's you,' he went to the account manager with her email and sanctioned her leave. But she could leave for home only after three more days. It was to wait until Sandhya got leave and she could see her off to her parents' house in Himachal that she stuck around.

When Rithu walked into their home unexpectedly the next morning, her father Kurian Sir and her mother Mamma Lally were taken aback. They were worried that she had come back home the same way she had gone away, casually rejecting, for nonsensical reasons, all the job offers she had got from Bangalore, Hyderabad and even from Panjim, which was not far from home. 'If that is the case, dear daughter Rithu, without getting you married to someone, there is no way we are going to allow you to leave this house and go off anywhere', her father declared upon seeing her.

But it was only when she explained things in detail that they found out about Midhun's death. They were genuinely shocked. Theirs was no pretense. They had known him well. It was on the same day five or six months ago that all of them had turned up in Kurian Sir's Jose Villa in the morning, without any prior warning.

'These fellows have been saying for a long time that they want to bathe at the beaches of Goa. When we got a sudden holiday, we did not think twice. We just came down. Thought we'd give Mamma a surprise. We will not trouble you in any way, other than making you miss your service this Sunday. Food is not a problem for them,' Rithu had justified their intrusion thus. They continued to be in Jose Villa for the next four days. All of them, men and women, camped in the kitchen to make dosas in the morning, cut chicken for lunch and roll chapatis for dinner. At intervals, they went to the beaches to bathe and play. Took countless selfies at Dona Paula and Aguada Fort. Stood stunned seeing the architecture of old Portuguese churches. Critiqued idol worship standing in front of the mortal remains of St. Francis Xavier laid out in the Basilica of Bom Jesus. Empathized standing amidst the ruins of massive monasteries. Saw the secret pathways from the residences of the priests to the nunneries, and happily decided that all this must be the punishment that God gave them for their revelry. Hopped on to the Jhankar ferry and travelled up and down aimlessly. Experienced the thrill of a speedboat. Danced with a pot-bellied Punjabi on the dance floor of a tourist boat. Sat on the terrace in the night and downed local feni that Kurian Sir had secretly sourced for them. Roamed the streets until midnight on a high. Snacked on masala peanuts. Ate pork shawarma. Drank ginger lemon juice. Joined the locals to sing *Ganpati Bappa Morya* during the Ganesh Festival. Danced on the streets. And then, sometime in the night, trooped into the same room, spread a mat on the floor and went to sleep hugging each other.

These were important days for Rithu. It was on one of those days that she and Ragesh disclosed their love for each

other, which hitherto had been confined to the corners of
their hearts. Another day, after they had all left, she hinted
of her love to Mamma Lally, who said, 'Ayye, that white
pandi who wears round glasses? There's that other guy, that
Malayali. I would not have objected if it were him. I like him
a lot.' It was none other than Midhun that Rithu's Mamma
liked. After that, whenever she called from Delhi, though
both of them maintained a meaningful silence about Ragesh,
Mamma Lally always asked about Midhun. And talked about
him a lot. It was not surprising that the sudden news of his
death shocked them.

9

That night, Kurian Sir asked Rithu a question. 'Can I give you some work to help you take your mind off the memories?' Kurian Sir probably thought that it would be a change for Rithu, who seemed to be lost in thought about Midhun, with a book open in front of her as though she were reading, with the headphones on her ears as if she were listening and with the TV on as though she were watching. If it had been any other occasion, she would have climbed on to her scooty and escaped saying, 'No, that is not why I hopped on a train and came here', and then hung around with her old friends by the beach until midnight. But now, sitting cooped up in the house without even the heart to call them and let them know that she was in town, Rithu thought that this might be a good idea.

Kurian Sir entrusted her with the task of translating a few news stories that had appeared in *Diário de Noite*, a newspaper published in Goa during the time of the Portuguese. This was because he was aware of Rithu's proficiency in Portuguese, given that she had studied it in school and college. She took it up saying that Papa had different crazy projects at different times. She completed the assignment within the next four to five days, much faster than was expected from her, and handed it over to her father. It was only then that she had an inkling of the nature of the new madness that her father had taken on. Kurian Sir was writing the biography of Alvares, the high priest who, about a hundred years ago – when the Portuguese and, through them, the Catholic Church were continuing their dictatorship – had faced severe rejection and torture for walking out of the Church and for opposing their dictatorial behaviour. What Rithu had translated were news stories about Alvares – his death, public viewing, funeral cortège, burial and tributes. The first thing that amazed her was how and from where her father had managed to dig up all this after so many years. The second thing that amazed her, from what little she could glean from the newspaper articles, was that such a man had lived in this town.

In spite of his workload at the Fisheries Department, after chasing many insane, half-abandoned hobbies like the anthurium garden on the terrace, mushroom cultivation, fish breeding, rabbit farming, painting, studying magic, soap manufacturing and so on, Kurian Sir had his own reasons for stepping into the whole new space of writing a biography. It was when he had landed in Panjim before taking up a job that he discovered the tomb of Alvares in the municipal cemetery of St. Inez. The tomb of this venerable man, who passed away in 1923, lay lost amid the dense undergrowth, undiscovered by anyone. Before long, his mortal remains were moved to another church and that was declared a pilgrimage centre. It was the feeling that the world still really did not know enough about this man that suddenly led to the writing of the biography.

Rithu had also heard Mamma Lally's divergent point of view: 'None of that is the reason, Rithu. It is after praying to that holy spirit on his knees that he got a good job in the Fisheries Department and got a beautiful wife like me. This writing experiment in his old age is just a form of thanksgiving.'

Whatever be the reason, for the first time in her life, Rithu was impressed by a project taken up by her father and made a mental note that she should read the biography when it was done and ready. Just as there were no restrictions on expressing opinions openly to each other in her house, they also did not fight shy of praising each other when it was deserved. For the same reason, she praised her father's project during dinner that night. And reserved copies of the biography in advance for her friends to read.

For a moment, Kurian Sir felt a sliver of hope that it might be possible to get back their daughter who had moved away from their way of thinking and their beliefs.

10

The next morning, Rithu got a call from Pastor Philip. The call was to complain about the fact that the three of them had taken leave and vanished at the same time. Naturally, after many days, Midhun, his life, fate, God's will and everything filled her conversation with disappointment. The pastor told her that human life was fraught with trials and tribulations and that those who had come into the fold of faith should never falter. Not only that, if people who were not yet firmly entrenched in their faith stayed away from the fold for several days, they would become prone to doubts and temptations – so rather than just while away her vacation, he asked Rithu to return immediately and engage in missionary work of some kind. By then, he was not complaining, nor was he advising; Pastor Philip's voice was clearly reprimanding.

That disturbed her. Nobody had scolded her that way before. Rather, she had not allowed anyone to scold her. And she'd always had a retort for the few people who had scolded her in the past. So she was amazed that she did not utter a single word while the pastor was being tough with her, worrying that she had become someone she was not.

In that sorrow, Rithu suddenly felt like calling Ragesh. And call she did. 'Honestly, Rithu, if someone tells me that there is nothing like telepathy, I will kill them,' Ragesh exclaimed as soon as he picked up the phone. 'I had just typed your name on my mobile to call you,' he said. 'Telepathy, Rithu, is that one skill which man lost or forgot to master at that stage of his development when he invented language. In spite of that, everyone still has this skill in varying degrees. When we think of someone very intensely, some invisible wave reaches out to them.'

Rithu did not bother to refute that. Instead, she asked, 'Why were you thinking so intensely about me?'

'Oh, that. My hand brushed against your ring and got cut for the thirteenth time,' he replied.

'For how long have I been asking you to throw it away? I will buy you a gold ring if you want,' she said angrily.

This was not an issue of gold or the desire to wear a ring at all. More than all that, Ragesh had an emotional attachment to that ring. This was a trinket that Rithu had abandoned after a swim-fest on the beaches of Goa, saying it had lost its colour. 'In that case, I want it,' Ragesh had said and worn it on his finger. Though his friends had teased him about the 'fake female ring', he had not abandoned it. That was the first time he had expressed his love for Rithu. Though she demanded that he throw the ring away when its sharp stone cut his hand twelve times, he refused to do so, just as he did the thirteenth time.

It was after talking to him for a while that Rithu told him about Pastor Philip's call.

'I think so too,' Ragesh said. 'I too am being plagued by unnecessary thoughts out here. Why did God do this to the meekest man in our group? What then is the meaning of the faith that we found and the prayers that we pray? What is it that He, who promises to give everything that one asks for, is trying to say? How can Appa and Amma, as atheists who have not walked into faith, continue to live more happily than us? If you stay at home, your doubts will only increase. Must be the Devil's test. But I am unable to overcome this. If I stay on for a few more days, I feel like I might run away from faith. Pastor Philip is right. The Devil is behind us. In different forms, at different times. Now in the form of the memories of Midhun. Not just him, all my yesterdays have come back to haunt me. I'm tired, Rithu. I will go back to Delhi in two days. I must complete the remaining part of my missionary work during these holidays. To be honest, it is also to tell you this that I was going to call you. But you called before that. That means that God and you have understood my mind. When are you starting for Delhi? Let me know.'

Before Rithu could say anything, Ragesh hung up.

11

They gathered every Saturday evening in the name of Christ, in a second-floor apartment on Mandir Marg. To sing songs. To pray. To read the Bible. To listen to the Gospel. Theirs was a small fellowship that had about fifty to sixty people in its fold – 'the explorers', 'the beginners' and 'the ones who returned'. One of the many fellowships in Delhi – small, intense and full of goodness.

'I have been successful in shepherding hundreds of people into faith over the last thirty-two years. I am content with that. But many people who were with me started other fellowships and went their own way. Let what is good happen. It's enough if everyone is with Christ.' This is what the founder of the fellowship, Pastor Ko Hee-sung, used to say. It was when he retired and went back to his motherland Korea, that Pastor Sam Philip took over the responsibility. To assist Pastor Philip and to lead the Hindi service, Pastor Shanu and Pastor Jeromy Sundar were now part of the pastoral team.

After Pastor Philip took over, major changes took place in the fellowship. The long-standing relationship with the Hong Kong prayer group was broken off and a new relationship with a fellowship in Philadelphia was established. Home groups as well as the charity initiative called 'Sahayak' for children and women were started recently. As part of this, the members of the fellowship had to visit the slums of Delhi at least once a month. Those who failed to do so were reprimanded by Pastor Philip. 'Finding justice, standing up for the oppressed, taking charge of the orphans, taking care of the widows – these are things the fellowship stands for, our slogans. Everyone needs to participate in this. When it comes to this, there is no difference between the explorer and the beginner. There will be no difference. And it will not be allowed.'

There were only eight to ten people in the home group that met at Sandhya's flat every Wednesday. Sandhya, Rithu, Ragesh and a few neighbouring families. That's all. Small, intense and full of goodness, as Pastor Shanu would say. But after the common service on Saturdays, Pastor Philip used to chide them openly, saying that they were the home group that were the most backward when it came to social service. 'No one who has furthered their interests and left the fellowship has gone far,' he'd say. 'What is each person's plan to meet targets?' he would ask everyone harshly. 'One who has a debt to pay has no right to ask for anything in the presence of Christ. So before you complete writing your prayer and hand it over, please remember this,' he used to threaten.

'Before we get scolded next, we should reform, Sandhya. We should get at least a few rogues to join the fellowship, even if it is just to escape from this incessant blame game,' Rithu used to mutter every day. But how? There was no time to go in search of anyone after work.

There was an understanding between the fellowship and its members. After a person completes his education, becomes a believer and a full-fledged member, he has to bring a minimum of two people into the fellowship. This was the programme designed a long time ago by Pastor Ko. This was how the ministry grew.

'This is like the money-chain of our youth, Rithu', Kurian Sir later ridiculed it.

'Papa will only feel that way. From the day he was born, he belonged to a faction that could not even bring one person into its fold. But this is missionary work.' Rithu justified it as 'missionary work'. It was not that Kurian Sir did not have a retort for this. He kept quiet because it was through this fellowship that his daughter had got an acceptable job in an acceptable company with an acceptable salary. The fellowship too had such a path. Find employment of some kind for its members through its network of contacts. This was also a project designed by Pastor Ko. He was close to the CEOs of many MNCs that were headquartered in Korea. In those days, if you joined the fellowship, you were assured of a job somewhere. Hundreds of people had obtained very good jobs this way. Pastor Ko used to say, 'Security and prosperity are the assurances given to people with faith. It is not just about spiritual but also about physical sustenance. One who has joined the fellowship should be different from all others. The change he has undergone should be quite visible to the world.' It was not just Rithu and Sandhya – Midhun too had landed his job through the fellowship.

12

Ragesh's standpoint created another problem for Rithu. How could she go back after announcing that she was on leave for three weeks? She thought she would call Sandhya, but she was out of reach. She walked around the house not knowing what to do. She thought of stepping out for a bit – but quite unexpectedly, Kurian Sir had taken the scooty to go meet someone in Karmaly. She checked her Facebook – but nobody she knew was available to chat. Frustrated, she picked up a book from her father's collection and started reading. A way of doing away with the worry of not being able to take a decision. She thought about Dr Samuel's one-line advice: 'There is a way. The way is on its way.' Reading was her way of waiting for that way. It was only when she reached page thirty-seven of this path that Rithu realized that she had read this book before. She distinctly remembered reading, 'This love was my punishment. God's curse. Tough. And painful, like the edges of a rock clawing at your heart. But I was really enamoured of it. Because love is love. There is nothing to substitute it.' So what about the thirty-seven pages that passed before? Why did she not remember a single line from

those pages? Was memory at fault or the book, that it did
not offer anything memorable until then? Whatever it was,
that was the end of her reading. It was just as she was leaving
Kurian Sir's room that she saw a few notes and scribbles on
his table related to his new project. Out of curiosity, she read
one note.

'It was a time when most of the land in the villages of Panjim,
the nearby Taleigao, Santa Cruz and Ribandar, was saline and
marshy. A time when distributing clean water was a challenge.
A time when infectious diseases spread. A time when plague,
smallpox, typhoid and cholera claimed the lives of many. At
a time when the sick were being abandoned because of a lack
of medicine, a lack of caregivers and the fear of catching the
contagion, it was Pastor Alvares alone who stepped forward
fearlessly to take care of them. He went from door to door,
tending to patients. He took the sick people who had been
abandoned on the streets to his house. He carried the critically
ill to far-flung hospitals. He cleaned wounds that looked
disgusting. He cleaned the excrement and phlegm of patients
with his own hands. He buried the dead. He took to begging
to feed those he had sheltered in his house. Once a merchant
spat into his begging bowl. "This is for me; now please give me
something for the poor," is what Pastor Alvares said. It was
such a man that the Portuguese authorities excommunicated.
Imprisoned. Tortured. And accused of defending freedom
and speaking against injustice. If he had acknowledged the
Portuguese authorities, he could have enjoyed all the comforts

of the ministry. But Alvares was different in that he rejected all this.'

Rithu felt a current travel through her, just as the lone tree atop a hill feels a bolt of lightning travel through it. She did not have the wherewithal to process or understand this something that she felt. This something that made her feel that life as it had existed until yesterday was not life. This something that made her realize that the history of this city through which merriment flows had contained lives such as these and that she was breathing the same air that they had breathed. This something like an island that suddenly rose up from the sea to look at the sky.

These lines would perhaps not have had such an impact on Rithu if they had been written by an unknown person about a faraway city and its people.

Go she had to. As quickly as possible. What Ragesh said was true. Pastor Philip's admonishment was true. These days were not to be whiled away. Everyone was responsible for continuing the work that certain people had started a long time ago. She too was a link in the chain. God had singled her out for it. When she left Kurian Sir's room, Rithu had decided that she would go back to Delhi.

13

On her way back to Delhi, it was only after she crossed Bhopal that Rithu managed to get Sandhya on the phone.

'Don't you know that there is no signal in our house at the foot of the hills? It's only when I step out that I get a signal, that too a weak one. I had switched the phone off because I did not want to take calls,' Sandhya said indifferently.

'Pastor Philip already called me thrice today saying that you are not reachable. Come down quickly. It's not in Delhi but in our loneliness that Midhun will haunt us. Don't cancel your leave. We'll do something else. I have a few things in mind in connection with our charity,' Rithu tried to encourage her.

Sandhya did not say if she would come or not. 'I'll call you later,' she said and hung up.

Rithu called Ragesh immediately and asked, 'Where have you reached?'

'It took me some time to get a ticket. I'm still on my way. Passed Ramagundam, reaching Balharshah,' he said, sitting in a Gareeb Rath train, watching an internationally renowned evangelist speak.

Honestly, she came to know that there was a place called Balharshah only then. She felt ashamed and enlightened. How could she have lived here for twenty-three years without knowing this? Why did she not know this land? She had heard of Ramagundam a long time ago. Her father used to speak about the thermal power plant there in relation to electricity and power-cuts. But Balharshah. Where was that? Curious name. Balharshah … Balharshah … Like the name of a beautiful girl. She repeated the name, smiling. There were so many such places that she did not know of, that she had never heard of. She thought of the nostalgia a few places had evoked in her as she passed by them on the way to Sandhya's house once. Panipat, Kurukshetra, Ambala, Patiala, Chandigarh, Ludhiana, Jalandhar. Places that brought to fore the kings, the wars and the struggles from history books. Rithu had felt the same joy when she travelled past Jhansi and Mathura on her first trip to Delhi – the joy of knowing that places from the past existed in more or less the same way today.

In the meantime, the third call from Mamma Lally came in. Rithu saw the call and was angry. 'Mamma, I am not travelling in a helicopter or anything. This is an ordinary Indian train. It will reach on time. And if it derails on the way, you will see it on the news on TV. Keep watching.' She hung up angrily. How on earth did people travel without talking to each other when there were no pagers or mobiles? She was amazed that even Mamma, who had lived in those times, could not help but call all the time.

Before Rithu reached Delhi, Sandhya called to say that she was waiting for the bus in Bhuntar and would reach Delhi the next morning. The only worry that Rithu had then was how Sandhya would deal with a Delhi that did not have Midhun in it.

PART THREE | *Kasol*

14

Sandhya too was thinking the same thing as she waited for the Volvo to Delhi. About Midhun. About a Delhi without Midhun. And more of the Delhi with Midhun in it.

Sandhya had stepped out with her daughter, who was bored with her hostel mess, for pizza. It was a public holiday that came right in the middle of a hectic week. Thinking that she would also take care of a bit of shopping, she walked into a mall. Later, it was when she was sitting at the food court inspecting her bills again and again, upset that she had spent more time and money than planned on clothes and cosmetics, that a young man came and sat opposite her at the same table. It was much later that she would come to know that his name was Midhun. With all the other tables occupied, there was also no way she could have avoided him. In the next five minutes, her daughter became friends with him. She gave him French fries. She got a bite of her favourite chicken mayonnaise sandwich in return. Knowing that the way to the mother is often through the daughter, Sandhya ignored this exchange. She stayed focused on WhatsApp, Facebook and her phone calls. But in the middle of it, she replied to a comment of his, 'The glasses are okay – but you need to change the watch on your wrist urgently. It looks like a man's watch. It does not suit your slim arm.' Her reply was rude, meant to hurt. If it had been anyone else, he would have gotten up and walked off. But Midhun made light of the whole thing by saying, 'Bhabhi, why are you getting so worked up? If there is anything wrong in what I said, you can yell at me.' What she felt then for this young brat was the affection one would feel towards a younger brother. From there, it did not take much time for it to become a conversation without formalities. To Sandhya's question, 'What are you doing now in Delhi?' he replied, 'Should I answer in five minutes or thirty?' and then went on to tell his Delhi story in six minutes. Though totally improbable, they parted exchanging phone numbers. But they were not really parting then. She had no clue that they were parting temporarily, to be one again.

15

It was improbable that Sandhya would have read Marcel Proust. But he would have read Sandhya. Which is why he wrote many years ago about Sandhya walking from a scene in real life into a memory. Proust, in *Remembrance of Things Past*, says that we keep walking back into memory not just from the sense of sight, but also from the senses of smell, hearing, touch and so on. It was Midhun, the avid reader, who introduced that name to Sandhya. It was because she thought of Midhun that she thought of Proust. Without knowing a thing about what he had written.

Sandhya used to say, 'Midhun, if there is one single reason why I dislike you, it is because you are a reader. I hate books, Midhun. The reason is not books. But him. He was an avid reader. So I hate books. I hate reading. I hate everything that he likes. If I could work up so much hatred in just two years, you can imagine what kind of a person he must have been. We can understand ordinary men, Midhun. Morons. They have only a limited awareness of life. Their life probably starts and ends with money. But after reading day and night and after preaching to the community endlessly about women's empowerment, you should have seen the way he behaved at home. Then you'd understand what kind of a hypocrite he was. Which is why I took the decision to leave the house while he was reading. In the excitement of having read a book, he came to talk to me about it once. The strangest thing was that it was about the beauty of married life. In between, he kept saying that we should go on a tour. I was quietly preparing to leave at that time. And I left the house for good that evening. He probably would have smarted at the ridiculousness of the situation. At least, I hope he did. If I could not have inflicted at least that much pain, I would not be me, Midhun.'

Sandhya wondered at the way she had gently breezed out of a marriage which her family had conducted with great hope and celebration six years ago. In reality, it was not a book that made her walk down memory lane. It was just that what she saw reminded her of Midhun, his love for books and a conversation that they had had. Memories are like that. They do not have a sequence. They jump, flow, deviate and break off as they please. From the window seat of the Volvo, Sandhya saw a bike overtake her bus at high speed. And the biker's flat black helmet.

16

One of Midhun's biggest dreams was to own a Harley Davidson. Whenever he saw one, he would caress it, take a selfie with it, find out more about it – all this fascinated him.

'Let me save a decent amount. I will get myself one,' he would always tell Sandhya. 'I will drive down the mud roads of my mother's village and the roads between the hills of your Himachal for hours on end, with you holding on to me, hugging me from behind.' That would always remind her of Uncle Carlos, who would take her for long rides when she was a kid. She would never forget the mist-laden trips she made to Rohtang Pass on the back of his bike. Uncle Carlos was a paying guest who used to come and stay in their outhouse three or four times a year. He would be there for a month or two during the tourist season. At other times, he would go back within a week's time. He would never say where he was coming from or where he was going to. Other than the fact that he handed over the rent on time, he did not socialize with Sandhya's parents. He was always friends with Sandhya, though. It was during her rides with Uncle Carlos that she had first heard of a place called Goa and its beaches. She had never imagined that years later she would have a friend from Goa with whom she would go swimming. Such is life. A polluted river that upsets expectations and convictions to flow in the least expected way.

Once when Rithu visited, Uncle Carlos was in Sandhya's outhouse. Sandhya's beautiful house was in a valley filled with pine and apple orchards, in a village called Shat, just before Kasol, on the way from Manikaran to Bhuntar. The vast expanse of apple and pomegranate orchards around lent the house great beauty. 'And gave us our daily bread too,' Sandhya said later. Rithu sat and had a long conversation with Uncle Carlos who was from her own home state but, after leaving a very long time ago, now only came back occasionally as a visitor. In the end, he offered her a bike ride. 'Go right ahead. You will never forget this ride', Sandhya encouraged her. There was a curious thing that happened on that ride. On the deserted road to Kasol, there stood a beautiful woman with a bag. Sensing something wrong, Uncle Carlos parked his bike and found out that the girl, who had come there on her honeymoon, had quarrelled with her husband and left the hotel. He managed to talk her out of her anger, got her to ride double on the pillion, dropped her at her hotel and then continued the journey. 'If you were not here, I would have flown away with her. I would have shown her all of Kasol before dropping her back,' said Uncle Carlos, speeding along the dangerous road between the mountains. 'You're way past your retirement age. Why don't you leave young girls alone and pick someone your age?' Rithu taunted him from behind.

'How old do you think I am?' Uncle Carlos asked, laughing louder than the sound of the bike.

'What's the great mystery? Sixty. Max sixty-five,' said Rithu without a shadow of doubt, looking at his taut muscles and wrinkle-free face.

'You know how to praise a man. Now listen. This April, I turned eighty-two.' Rithu touched his muscles. They had the firmness of forty.

'How did you land up here in these mountains from the beaches of Goa?'

'Like everyone says, that's a story. I was marketing hotels in Goa. I was fascinated with riding bikes from way back then. I had an old Yezdi. Once, a Portuguese lady who had set out to see India asked me if I could go with her as a guide. I did not think twice. Just hit the road. This was before you and Sandhya were born. After wandering quite a bit, we camped in Kasol. The Portuguese left, but Carlos did not. Taking foreign women out on bike rides became my job. Kasol was full of them. They liked wrapping themselves around these muscles. I would show them the glorious mountains of Himachal on a bike. At times, I would take them to Dharamshala. To show them Buddhas. At times, I would take them to Shimla, to show them the lake. At times to Kashmir, to show them what natural beauty was all about. I would take them to the sanyasis in Rishikesh and get them good quality marijuana. Take them to Rajasthan and get them to taste bhang. At times, we would end up doing all of India. Bike. Marijuana. Sex. These were my favourite things. I gave these abundantly to everyone who needed them. I still have my first job of riding bikes. Stopped the other two. Tired. I get defeated by female energy and marijuana. I once believed firmly that this was what life was all about. So I forgot to get married. I realize the loss only now. But it's too late. What Dr Weir Mitchell said is true – I'm in the arctic loneliness of age. It is only now, after getting to this point in life, that I understand the burden of loneliness. One should get married. Only then will life be complete. The completeness that one gets from this, one will not get from anything else.'

When she heard Uncle Carlos say that, Rithu was reminded of her dear friend Sandhya telling her that she was on the brink of a divorce. Nobody was aware of that then. Not even her parents.

17

They met long after they got to know each other over long telephone calls. By then, they were already like siblings. It had not been long since Sandhya had joined the new MNC. That was the time Midhun, after completing his degree programme in Delhi University, was waiting for the results of his PG entrance test, while working part-time as the PA cum-Secretary-cum-cook-cum-servant of the Bengali professor Jithin Das. He had got away from work that day to meet his new, unexpectedly found friend from the city, Sandhya.

'I still laugh when I think of the day on which I first met you', Midhun had said then. 'I walked into the food court all excited, after getting my first salary from Jithin Das. That's not the fun part. Do you know where I went after stuffing myself with hamburgers and Pepsi? To participate in a May Day rally. I have a roommate called Sajan. He was the one who pulled me into it. The irony of it always makes me laugh. I too became one of those new-gen types who wears Che Guevara T-shirts and goes to the temple.'

That day, they walked endlessly through the streets of Palika Bazaar. 'Let those who have money wear originals. I need only these duplicates,' said Midhun, as he picked up a bunch of seconds. Sandhya, in the meantime, picked up a few good pieces meant for women. 'Take this. You can give these to your beautiful mother when you go home.'

'I don't buy clothes for anyone,' said Midhun. 'Attire, like love, is a very personal choice. It is better not to measure our love with it.'

As Sandhya pulled out a blanket from her bag to fight the cold draught of the Volvo, she remembered that it was not because she did not have a fitting reply to what he said that she had kept quiet, but because she did not want to get into a futile argument with that kid. Then, from the other side of time, she gave Midhun a reply. Knowing fully well that it would never reach him. 'Midhun, I am tired of all your logic. Why are you always like this? You need to be a bit more optimistic. We will love the clothes that our loved ones buy for us. We place their likes way above ours. Don't we? Take this blanket that I just wrapped around me, for instance – I like this very much. Why is that? Only because you gifted it to me that day.'

They then got into a small dhaba called 'Al Kabab – Mughlai Food' and had chapati and chana. Sandhya had not taken leave to wander around thus. She had just requested time to step out for a bit from her new job at the MNC. She needed to go meet her lawyer at eight in the evening. She thought of taking Midhun along with her. It was not because she was scared of moving around in this city without being accompanied by a male. She just wanted to have someone to talk to. This was the time she was going through the last phase of her divorce.

'The court proceedings are more or less over. Now I need to wait for six months. In between, there's a counselling session just for formality. Once that is also over, I can do away with the knot that my family tied,' Sandhya said on the way back.

'To be honest, Midhun, I am really angry. To get a divorce, look at the formalities that the state imposes on us. Court case, lawyer, police, battle, cross-examination, counselling … why is the state this concerned only when one wants to walk out of the contract called marriage? If so, they should make it mandatory for everyone to go through a set of hurdles in order to get married. Forget that, this counselling they talk about – they should insist that the two people involved and their parents participate in a session before they marry. If they do this, many marriages here will not happen. But now, the family and the representatives of God on earth get together and dump a stranger on you without any consideration or thought. Almost like saying: now you suffer. I'm fed up, Midhun. I will not stick my neck into another marriage no matter how boring people say living alone can be.'

When Sandhya said that, she had no idea that the day she would fall deeply in love with this youngster Midhun, who was five years younger than her, was not too far away.

18

Sandhya first stepped into Midhun's life by latching on to his excuse that he smoked to overcome the intense cold of the city. She used the authority and love of a sister to do so. She forcibly removed the smouldering cigarette from his lips and stuck an electronic cigarette in its place saying, 'If you can't stop, then smoke this. Instead of the smoke that will singe your lungs, enjoy the virtual smoke of vaping.'

Midhun was totally convinced. It was a time when he himself was trying to get out of the habit that he had acquired quite recently. Some habits are difficult to get rid of on your own. It requires persistent scolding that can't be ignored. From people who truly love you.

Sandhya's second intrusion was when she found out that Midhun was lying about the fact that he was waiting for the results of the PG entrance test. She somehow discovered that he had lazed around in the final year and had three more papers to clear. 'I will have to tell that poor woman this,' Sandhya threatened Midhun, picking up the phone to call his mother for the first time. But she was not that cruel.

She spoke of other things and hung up. It would be more correct to say that his mother hung up in a hurry after a brief conversation, half in Hindi and half in English. 'This is your last chance. You have to clear the papers in the next attempt', Sandhya chided.

It was to find out how XOXO came to symbolize kisses and hugs that Midhun called Sandhya one night. It really was not an excuse to call. Being a person from a middle-class family in Kerala with a regular education, who had been uprooted and thrown into the metro-English of Delhi, he had a pile of such doubts. What is the correct meaning of 'dead in the water'? How is 'cicerone' pronounced? Is a bank 'open' or 'opened'? Is it true that it is from a light-hearted misspelling 'orl korrekt', published on the second page of the *Boston Morning Post* of 23 March 1839, that the word 'OK' was born? What is a 'burr hole'? What is 'voluntourism?' Is 'Twitterati' the youngest word in English? More than the fact that he had no one else to ask these questions, what Midhun tried to overcome through Sandhya was the inferiority complex that he would have had by exposing his lack of awareness to others. In short, he felt that level of ease with her. But she did not know the answers to many of these questions. 'Midhun, I lived in a far more backward village than you did. The only thing I gained from that man was that I moved from the remote mountains to Delhi', Sandhya had said about her marriage. 'You're mad, Midhun. I am living proof that you can live for twenty-six years and work in an MNC for two years without knowing all this. Go read your textbooks and score well in the papers that you failed in,' she scolded him.

'Mad! Yes, you are right. But doesn't everyone have something like this?' Midhun justified himself. 'Listen, Bhabhi. If you heard that there were scientists who wandered around the mountains of Jerusalem in the belief that the sound waves produced by Jesus Christ over two thousand years ago, during his Sermon on the Mount, are still reverberating somewhere there, what would you call them – researchers or madmen?'

Sandhya gave up, saying, 'I can't argue with you.'

When they met next, Midhun gifted her one of his favourite books. Nikos Kazantzakis's *Report to Greco*. Actually, Midhun had a second-hand copy of the book. It was something he had stolen from a bookstore the other day. This habit, or perhaps deviance, had developed in him following his obsession with reading. He would want to buy every good book that he came across. Because the pocket money from home and the paltry salary from Jithin Das would not allow this, he would steal. Is it not to read? Midhun believed that this was not a sin.

'Midhun, don't you know my aversion to books and reading? Then why did you give this to me?' Sandhya asked.

'To get rid of that aversion once and for all. I am an avid reader. If you love me, you should love reading. I will be reading this book for the third time, starting tomorrow. Read along with me. We'll share till where we have reached every night before we go to sleep.'

Sandhya did not say if she loved him or not. Instead, she started reading the book from the next day. In between, she would call and ask, 'Where have you reached?'

'I'm on page sixteen,' he would say.

'Oh, don't read so fast. I just reached the eighth page,' she said.

'Okay, I'll stop. Tell me when you have reached page sixteen, Bhabhi,' he replied.

'Oh! That's such a beautiful line … on page fifteen. "The cross is the only path to resurrection. There is no other path." I was transfixed when I read that. There are people who write like this?' Sandhya would say, calling him in the middle of the night, lost in the excitement of reading the book. They read together. The process turned out to be more interesting than fiction. In the days that followed, they progressed together from page sixteen to page twenty-two, from page twenty-two to forty-five, from there to ninety-two and then to one hundred thirty-two. But when he reached page hundred forty-four, unlike in his previous readings, he froze at one line. Though Sandhya had gone way past, he could not move from that page. Like a calf that has fallen into quicksand, he struggled to swim. He could not pull himself out. Nor did he drown. He came down with fever.

Sandhya could not understand what he had read that had affected him so much. It was after asking him repeatedly that he shared the line with Sandhya. 'If a woman calls you to sleep with her and you do not go, you are damned. God does not forgive this. You will be placed with Judas at the very bottom of hell!' She cut the call without saying anything.

Very late that night, a message bearing a beating heart and a red kiss came flying and landed on Midhun's WhatsApp. It was sent by Sandhya – who, until then, had been just his Bhabhi.

19

The Volvo had stopped in front of a Punjabi dhaba for dinner. A Daler Mehndi song was playing loudly. And even louder were the voices of the people waiting to eat. Sandhya was not hungry. She asked herself if she should have two rotis and chana masala, and replied to herself in the negative. She went to the washroom and returned to her seat in the bus. Though the old man sitting next to her removed his earphones in an attempt to start a conversation, Sandhya ruthlessly refused to oblige. She thought of Midhun. All she wanted to do was think of him. The Midhun who accepted her invitation solely because he had no desire to be with Judas at the very bottom of hell. The Midhun who used to pull her close to his heart and cry out, 'I want you forever and a day, Sandhya.'

'During my childhood, I had a thousand dreams about life,' Sandhya told Midhun one day. 'Becoming an actor, a dancer, teacher, doctor, woodcutter, laundry lady, maid, patient, nomad, driver, princess, why, even a widow, a murderer or a lesbian. But I never dreamt of a life like this, Midhun. With a boy like you. I've always wondered at the ease with which life defeats all our dreams.'

'Life is a football game between dreams and fate', Midhun had replied. 'Though we try to move forward constantly towards our dreams using our hard work, careful planning and savings, fate will circumvent everything and score a goal. What is most interesting is the fact that the goal will be scored from the most unexpected angle.'

Midhun was always like that. He had a reply for everything. Something that you couldn't counter or argue with and win. Listening to him speak, Sandhya often genuinely felt that he might become a great writer or a philosopher.

When the Volvo descended from the hills into the heat of Delhi, Sandhya thought of the last conversation they had had. Around that time, a book review Midhun had written was published by a prominent weekly. But in their carelessness, they had forgotten to give the byline. 'Don't make an issue of it,' Midhun had said. 'This is what Roland Barthes calls the "death of an author". We should look at this philosophically. Writing that goes beyond the writer. That is Midhun's writing!' It was after this that Midhun had the accident. His words had come true. 'Death of an author.' It was the death of an author who belonged to the future.

PART FOUR | *Chennai*

20

Ragesh had gone to enjoy the mehfil-e-mushaira of the Urdu poet Shiraz Ali. His poetry evenings were very famous. What was different about them was that his poems were never written in advance and never repeated. He was an instant poet who crafted his songs for each crowd differently. Each poem would be born just once and would die immediately thereafter. The tempo would be slow in the beginning. Using very ordinary lines and even more ordinary concepts at times. Making one wonder if the mere humming of someone who had no inclination towards verse would have been better. One might even feel angry, thinking that his fame was completely unwarranted and unjustified. But then, suddenly, the poem would take a turn and move into a plane that nobody could have seen coming. Like the kite that breaks away from your hand and soars magnificently into the blue sky, leaving you wonderstruck. These instant poems would turn out to be far deeper and more lyrical that the ones crafted painstakingly, rewritten many times over. And that is what drew the crowds towards Shiraz Ali. No one would forget the way he metamorphosed onstage into a divine madman, like a Sufi. Critics had tried to dismiss his poetry as distorted poetic prose, lacking meaning. But with each passing day, more and more people heard him. They were certain that, more than just the pleasure of listening, these poems offered many meditative moments. They did not pay any heed to the critics.

'Who knows if these lines were crafted earlier? One does tend to wonder if there is a clever strategy behind this,' Ragesh commented to a young man sitting next to him who was recording the poems.

'No. Never. I was a hardcore Shiraz Ali critic,' the young man said. 'Which is why I have been tracking him, attending the last forty-three performances of his. Not just in Delhi. But in many cities across India. I recorded every single one of them and listened to them repeatedly. I discovered with amazement and envy that he has not repeated a single line anywhere. Shiraz Ali is an ocean of poetry. The waves of this ocean will never tire you out with repetition. You can trust this poet. His poetry will never deceive.'

As they stepped out after an evening of poetry, the young man invited Ragesh to share a bottle of beer. He had a charming personality, and large sideburns, long hair and the eyes of Jesus Christ. Ragesh could not resist his invitation. It was the beginning of a friendship. The name of the young man was Kiran.

That was also when Kiran had decided to move out of Rohini West and was on the lookout for a room in Vishwavidyalaya so that he could continue with both his new part-time job and his research at the same time. 'There is no room on offer. But I can give you space to put a mattress,' promised Ragesh, as they parted after beer. Ragesh thought that this promise would be forgotten after the heat of the poetry and the cold of the beer dissipated. But before a week had passed, Kiran alighted bag and baggage at the Vishwavidyalaya metro station and called Ragesh.

'I feel like I have been in this space before,' is what Kiran said when he reached Ragesh's flat. 'I feel the same dread that Albert Schweitzer felt when he stepped into his cell, Ragesh,' he added, half in jest. Schweitzer recalls later that he first saw the room in a Van Gogh painting. That was the room in which Van Gogh spent four months living out his painful madness before he took his own life. Sitting in the Gareeb Rath from Chennai, Ragesh wondered if Kiran's dread had actually been a premonition.

21

Two friends studied law endlessly in one room, without any end in sight. In another room were two students of Delhi University. And then a room just for Ragesh. That was how the three-bedroom flat was shared. It was that room Kiran walked into as Ragesh's roommate. All the others were studious and busy. Ragesh had extended the invitation simply because he thought Kiran would be the kind of person with whom he could have a conversation and exchange ideas after coming back home from work. But that thought was totally misplaced. It took some time for Ragesh to understand that Kiran was a strange guy who would come only occasionally to the room at odd hours to either endlessly smoke grass or eat chilli bhajis. In spite of Ragesh's taking the liberty to advise him, scold him and even threatening to kick him out, Kiran paid no heed.

'This is my eleventh room in Delhi. With just the bare essentials that I own, it is not difficult for me to find another one. I am who I am. I don't think you should try to change me, Ragesh.' Kiran's words had a finality to them.

Kiran had heard Appan speak about how there was or is a policewoman called Kiran Baby or something like that. Despite being in Delhi, he was not aware of the fact that she had recently stepped into politics. It was new knowledge for Ragesh that even in Delhi, one could exist hearing and not hearing, knowing and not knowing the things that one liked to hear and know. Not just that. It was because Appan had been very impressed with her and her courage that Kiran had been named Kiran. Appan wanted his son to become a police officer like her. He had brought him up that way. Enrolled him for NCC and as a scout in school. When others played cricket, he was part of the parade in a corner of the playground. Just because of that, Kiran hated the thought of becoming a policeman. He stubbornly refused to go in that direction. He grew his hair long and sported large sideburns – things that were anathema to the force. And chose research as his favourite profession. Kiran was kicked out of home by an angry Appan. 'You can have dinner at this table the day you shave this head of yours.' No less stubborn than his father, the son neither rid himself of his hair and his sideburns, nor did he have dinner at that table. And he chose Delhi as his permanent base.

22

It was only when he reached Chennai that Ragesh metamorphosed into his parents' little boy and a pure brahmin wearing the sacred, consecrated thread. He would transform into a different person outside the boundaries of that city. A diehard fan of BBC. Not the famous news channel. Beef. Beer. Cricket. The last two might be forgiven by folks at home if there was just no other way out. But beef was unthinkable. He would be kicked out of the house. But Ragesh was like a tiger that has tasted salted human meat. It was during his hostel days in Bangalore that some Keralite, a Christian, started bringing beef in baked plantain leaves for him. He became a slave to that taste. He could not give it up. If it was not available, he would go in search of it. There was a time when he used to travel quite a distance to play cricket for a few local clubs in return for beef and beer.

It was when he reached Delhi that he really suffered. There was nobody to tempt him or buy beef for him. It was when he had managed to suppress his desire for beef like one suppresses lust, and had learnt to make do with just mutton, that Kiran entered his life. Ragesh had just happened to speak about his desire during a conversation, and Kiran came the next day carrying a large paper packet of beef fry. When Ragesh asked him where he had managed to get it from, Kiran replied lazily, 'Why do you want to know all that, my friend? What banned thing can't you get in this country? Banned book? Banned organization? Banned liquor? Banned movie? What is a bit of beef in comparison?'

Kiran had a talent like that. The talent to go anywhere and fish out anything and everything. Three days after he moved in, when he managed to discover the secret that the Punjabi's shop next door, on the street on which they had been living for three years, sold fresh grass, the news, to Ragesh and his flatmates, was like someone discovering a new planet. The degree students in the next room asked in passing during a conversation one night if it would be possible to get Sappho's *Isle of Lesbos*. It took Kiran just two weeks to get a photocopy of the book by messaging a Greek professor on Facebook, whom he had met once upon a time in Connaught Place! Ragesh just happened to mention that his neighbour and classmate Kokila had joined Lady Shri Ram as a junior lecturer. The very next day, Kiran came home with her mobile number and her address in Dilshad Garden. That was Kiran. Which is why, in no time, Kiran had endeared himself to not just everyone in that flat but also everyone who came to the dhaba on that street. It was more or less like that everywhere he went.

For the same reason, Kiran was the best roommate Ragesh could have had in that city. A genius in every way. Painting was one of Kiran's favourite hobbies. Even at that age, he had an amazing knowledge of painters and paintings. Ragesh understood how to appreciate art, thanks to Kiran. He learnt the differences between cubism, Dadaism and surrealism from Kiran. It was also Kiran who introduced him to the creations of Henry Matisse, Uttam Roy, Edvard Munch and Caravaggio. He had put up a framed copy of Picasso's *Nude with Drapery* next to his bed. Kiran's passion for Picasso's *The Young Ladies of Avignon* was beyond Ragesh's understanding.

Kiran, who was open to discussing anything and everything, did not disclose the topic of his research to Ragesh for a long time. Ragesh guessed that it might be something to do with painting.

Later, one day, fortified by the smoke from his grass, Kiran revealed that his research was not just about painting, but how it could be linked to neuroscience.

'There is a study that states that if we excite the mirror neurons in the front of our brain and numb our sensory system, we will be able to experience one man touching another, though both of them are far from us. I am researching how this can be used in the sex industry and pornography. The way to bodily experience a sexual encounter that one sees at a distance. Then we will be able to telecast pleasure. If I succeed, I will become greater than Kiran Bedi, Kiran Desai, Kiran More, Kiran Rao and Kiran Khan,' is what Kiran used to tell Ragesh, his roommate, all the while eating chilli bhajis. But Kiran could not realize his dream.

23

If one thing disturbed Kiran more than anything else, it was the fact that it was J.D. Salinger's *Catcher in the Rye* that inspired the religious fanatic Mark David Chapman to shoot and kill the great musician John Lennon. Because *Catcher in the Rye* was one of Kiran's favourite books. Ragesh had heard him speak about it endlessly to at least a hundred people. He had also spent his own money to buy copies of that book for the same number of people. His argument was that there were only a handful of books that could talk to the youngsters of every generation. John Lennon was also equally dear to him. Kiran also believed that we would have to wait another century for such a great talent to be born. But what disturbed him was that it was a murder that connected these two passions of his. It was John's statement that their band was more popular than Jesus that provoked Chapman. After shooting John Lennon five times, Chapman stood there until the police came, reading Salinger's novel.

Ragesh did not understand why Kiran brought this up without any reason during their conversation one night. But in the next minute, he spoke of Reshma. It was the first time he had mentioned a girl like that. It was difficult to believe that, amidst his mad research dreams, he could have found the time for someone else. 'There is a light and sound show in the evening at Akshardham. It started recently. I sold popcorn there briefly. Just for fun. Charity without any expense. I stopped when the novelty ran out,' Kiran said and went on to add that it was during that journey that he met Reshma. It was much later that Ragesh understood that it was not a mere acquaintance, but a love that was entrenched at the very bottom of his heart.

Ragesh came back to the present reality around him in the Gareeb Rath, almost as though he was afraid to dwell upon those days. He sat looking out of the window to ensure that memories did not come knocking again. He could not still his mind. He had to turn his mind's eye to something else. Ragesh was reminded of Javed Akhtar's poem which asks if time stands still like the moving trees that you see from a train and if we are the ones who are passing through. Could it be? Could fleeting time also be just an illusion like the fleeting trees? Is time standing still and are we just sightseeing travellers? If so, are we the victims of time? Actors in a pre-written play? People who don't have permission to change even a step on their own?

Just as it is said that someone who looks at us from beyond many light years will be able to see our past, just as it is said that the stars we see in the sky today are stars from the past, will someone standing beyond infinity be able to see our future? It's like saying that, as we travel, though we relate only to what we see on our side, someone who's above us can see all the way to the end of the path. Who am I? Why am I? How am I? How long has man been asking this to himself and God? It is unbearable that every generation ends up asking the same questions. It's time God gave up his silence. Enough God, enough. Deliver us from this darkness. Give us an answer to the question: Whose play are we enacting? It is not that I don't understand that it is as difficult for God to talk to man as it is difficult for man to talk to ants. It is high time you once again sent another person with the same intelligence and same language in our midst. God, the new world awaits not an innocent Christ, but a new Einstein. Someone who is equipped to explain the true meaning of our journey.

Ragesh imagined that the dead woke up as inhabitants of another planet light years away and could see our past, present and future through a telescope. And that Kiran was there, looking.

24

'There is no giant tree that grew thus far because it was watered every day. All the giant trees of today are plants that sourced what they needed using their own roots.'

It was when Kiran was expounding his philosophy very authoritatively, seated at the Punjabi dhaba next to the flat, that Reshma walked in there for the first time. That dhaba was a base for all the students of Vishwavidyalaya. They kept walking in and out at all times of the day and night. One could get anything there – from palak paneer, chicken masala, mutton roast, anda paratha, dal chawal, pani puri, samosa, momos and chole bhature to tea, coffee and sugarcane juice. Above the din and bustle, the constant conversations and the cigarette smoke, one could hear people screaming out their orders incessantly. It was in the midst of all this that Reshma walked in and said very loudly, 'Please stop talking. I have a very important question to ask you.' Like rain abating, the noise died down.

'One question. Somebody tell me the name of the Colombian footballer who was shot dead on the street because he scored a self-goal.' The rain did not start for a moment. Everyone was racking their brains for the answer.

'Andrés Escobar!' The answer came from the back bench in a soft voice. Everyone turned to look. It was Kiran who had answered nonchalantly, blowing out cigarette smoke.

'Oh! Thank God. I've been trying to find this out for so long.' Reshma went and sat opposite Kiran. 'You have a good memory,' she said. Kiran's lips hovered between a smile and a smirk. It was difficult to make out whether he had accepted the compliment or not.

'Honestly, that was only the prelude to my actual question – it is for the next question that I actually need an answer,' said Reshma. 'What was the name of the Italian player who, in the 1938 World Cup, dropped his shorts to distract the Brazilian goalie Walter before taking a penalty kick to score a beautiful goal? Do you know?' Kiran glared at her for a while.

'Honestly, this is not a joke. I could not possibly have asked this question to someone who did not even remember Escobar's name – hence the first question.' There was an innocence in Reshma's eyes that seemed to have caught Kiran's attention. In the same split second that Kiran said, 'Giuseppe Messa is the name of that shrewd player,' Reshma jumped up and planted a kiss on his cheek. Everyone in the dhaba was stunned. Kiran responded by asking, 'Is this how you kiss, girl – shouldn't I feel the wetness of your lips on my cheeks?,' and giving Reshma just such a kiss. Though she was proud of her impulsive action, the fact of the matter was that she had not expected such a reaction. Which is why she was startled. Kiran changed the topic by asking, 'What do you want from Giuseppe?'

'No, nothing. It was to complete a puzzle. See you then,' she said and breezed out of the dhaba. Her nonchalance was what captivated and conquered Kiran. But that happened because of a metro journey with her to Akshardham.

25

Somewhere between all this, one of the two degree students moved out and Kiran moved into their room. Ragesh was alone again. He was not upset because he too was looking for a way to escape the permanent stench of grass hanging in the room. Nikhil was the name of the degree student who stayed on in the second room. An absolute simpleton from Kerala. It was for him that Kiran had sourced a copy of *Isle of Lesbos* from the Greek professor. Though everyone thought that Kiran's company would be really suffocating for him, once they started living in the same room, there was a strong connect that developed between the two of them. Not only that, the Kiran-Reshma-Nikhil core group slowly established its presence in the dhaba. Even Ragesh was not part of it. And Ragesh was a bit sore about that. He was the person responsible for bringing Kiran to Vishwavidyalaya and giving him a room there, after all. Yet he was the one left out of Kiran's circle. He could not comprehend why. And for the same reason, he fell into the opposite camp. He added colour to every story that went around about the trio. But none of these affected them. The core group of three stood and fought together in all the debates and conversations that took place at the dhaba. Kiran's intelligence, Reshma's sharpness and Nikhil's inquisitiveness made them invincible. The camaraderie was not limited to just that. They went to the cinema, the park and the market together. There was more romanticism in that than in a Bollywood movie. Not only that, inspired by Édouard Manet's famous painting *The Luncheon on the Grass*, they went together to India Gate and took selfies (the two men in suits and she naked), which became a huge topic of discussion in social and other media. They even had to face a police case in connection with this. They rejoiced proudly. But Ragesh never understood where Nikhil stood in the relationship between Kiran and Reshma, or where Reshma stood in the relationship between Kiran and Nikhil.

It was when Ragesh saw Reshma walk out of Kiran's room one day, looking wounded and angry, that he realized that there was a problem in the relationship. Though he wanted to know what the problem was, he decided to respect their privacy and not ask. But in no time, the news spread like wildfire in the dhaba. It was not Ragesh who had let the cat out of the bag. Reshma had stopped coming to the dhaba. They also heard that she had moved out of Vidya Vihar. It was a torrent of stories from then on. For every debate they had lost in the dhaba, they took revenge by creating a new story. Kiran, Nikhil and Reshma were victims of this cruel game. Though Ragesh did not participate actively in this, he derived a kind of masturbatory pleasure out of it.

A few days later, Nikhil himself walked into Ragesh's room. He informed him that he had got admission for another course in Pune and that he was leaving Delhi immediately. So many people had come, stayed and gone after he had taken the flat. For Ragesh, Nikhil's departure was another such unimportant move. But it was anyone's guess that the departure was because of the stories that were going around connected to Reshma. It was all too much for a simpleton like Nikhil to bear.

'Kiran is more broken than we thought. If possible, save him. Get Reshma back for him. He cannot live without her.' Before leaving the room, Nikhil requested this of Ragesh. 'Let me see,' replied Ragesh, dismissively. Not only that, whenever he met Kiran later, Ragesh did not feel that the loss had any impact on him. He continued to visit the dhaba and participate in the debates. It was true that he did not have the same passion as he once had. But Ragesh felt that it did not deserve attention. What Ragesh did not notice was that, once in the flat, Kiran would just shut himself up in the room. Most of them thought that he would be smoking grass.

But it was not so. Behind that strong indifference, there was the tenacity of plans being hatched. It was only much later, when Reshma visited the flat with Rithu and told him, that Ragesh understood – Kiran had called Reshma that night, after all his plans were made, and had spoken to her at length. But it was all too late by then.

PART FIVE | *Delhi*

26

It was not for the first time that Rithu was going for charity work. She had participated happily in it many times after she had become a part of the fellowship. She had walked in and out of the homes of the poor in the lanes of the city, distributing clothes, medicines and food. Time permitting, neither she nor anyone in her home group had shown any reluctance in doing so. Which is why she did not understand why Pastor Philip had called on the morning of the day she landed in Delhi and told her with a hint of admonishment, 'The three of you *have* to be present at the programme that is being organized in Mayur Vihar the day after tomorrow.'

'Sandhya and Ragesh are on their way. We will be there,' she said and hung up.

Normally, it was Pastor Shanu who informed them of such things. Or an email would come. The call from Pastor Philip was unusual. She learnt later that it was not just her, Pastor Philip had also called Ragesh and Sandhya the same day. She pacified herself by thinking that this direct intervention could probably be because he realized the impact Midhun's death had on them.

But like never before, dissent and resentment were all that Rithu felt for the programme that happened after two days. Though it was called charity and all that, she saw it as a disturbing performance. Not only that, more than being a monthly programme of the fellowship, she felt that it was a programme designed to promote the Trinity Foundation.

The Trinity Foundation was a private enterprise created recently by Dr John Samuel, Pastor Sam Philip and Advocate Ram Manohar Varma. The stated aims of the foundation were to promote organ donation, find organ donors, create an extensive network of hospitals that could share information about organs available and solve the legal problems of organ donors and recipients. In just two years, Trinity reached a prominent position in the list of non-profit organizations working in the field of organ donation. It achieved this by conducting awareness classes for the public, camps for finding donors and recipients, charity work, the launch of a website, brochures, etc. It was Pastor Philip's leadership and his fellowship that were powering this venture. For all the programmes conducted by the Trinity Foundation, it was the foundation's members that did all the volunteering work. They were only happy to do so. But now, Rithu felt that the focus was only on the foundation and that the work of the fellowship was taking a back seat.

'Don't think unnecessary thoughts. This is the hangover of all the reading that you did on some old pastor. That's all,' Ragesh chided her. It wasn't as if she too felt the same way. But there had been a pastor in her city who had taken care of the genuinely poor, sick and abandoned people without any publicity or gain of any kind. It amazed her that someone could, in the name of Christ, do such selfless service without any reason, without any need to do so. The truth was that there were clear reasons why she and the others had joined the fellowship.

27

That was the night dream met life. Ragesh was blissfully sleeping off his tiring two-day train journey, after having relished his mother's curd rice which he had long been craving for. That's when good dreams came calling. He dreamt that he was travelling with his friends to a village in Kerala and that they had stopped at a local wayside restaurant to have food. And every plate kept in front of them had the same delicacy. Beef, roasted with lots of onion, exuding the fragrance of pepper and the glint of fresh coconut oil. And lots of toddy to drown it in. Even in that state of sleep, more water than in the Suez Canal flooded Ragesh's mouth. His greedy hand reaching out for food and his mobile ringing happened at the exact same time. Saying 'I'll be back soon,' Ragesh left the restaurant and his noisy friends to attend the call. It was one of his longstanding flatmates from Delhi, who kept studying law endlessly, on the other end of the line.

'There's an emergency in our room. You should get here as fast as you possibly can,' was the crux of the call. Though he asked what the matter was, there was no clear reply forthcoming. 'You are needed here. Come fast,' was what was repeated again. 'Okay, okay, I'll come,' said Ragesh and hung up. And then Ragesh went back to the restaurant and the food. His friends, who had finished almost half the food, asked him whose call that was.

'Our roommate – there is some emergency. He asked me to return to Delhi quickly,' Ragesh replied.

'Why hurry? You sit here,' they said, dissuading him. Ragesh fell for the temptation called beef and kept enjoying it until the end of the dream.

Ragesh remembered the dream quite well when he awoke. Better than something that had happened the previous day. Not only that, he felt the taste of that beef still lingering on his palate. If one dreams, it should be tasty dreams like this, he thought proudly. It was not that he had forgotten the call that came in between. But he was sure that that was part of the dream – until the next call came a while later. 'Have you started?' was the question from the other end of the line.

'Start? Where to? I just reached here yesterday,' said Ragesh, perplexed.

'So did you not understand what you were told last night?' the voice on the other side thundered. After that call, Ragesh sat stupefied for a minute and then checked the call list on his phone to discover that he had indeed spoken for one minute and thirty-three seconds at 2:47 in the night to the guy in Delhi who was studying law endlessly. Ragesh could not even imagine that man could thus marry dream and reality. He returned the call from Delhi. It was only then that he realized that during the night he had eaten his fill of beef, Kiran had committed suicide.

28

One day, during the phase when Ragesh was struggling to get over the trauma of Kiran's death, he went to Dr John Samuel's hospital. Though he was burdened with unbearable tension, insomnia, guilt and fear, it was not to treat any of these that he landed up there. Dizziness, vomiting, stomach pain, breathlessness, cough and chest pain had also latched on to him, weighing him down further. That was the time swine flu, and along with it panic, was spreading in the city. The day the death of two women – one in Dr Ram Manohar Lohia hospital and the other in Safdarjung – was announced as breaking news on TV and the lady reading the news listed out the symptoms, Ragesh decided to stop experimenting by self-medicating himself with paracetamol. Six people had died of swine flu that year. Two hundred and sixteen other cases were reported from within city limits. Wasn't that enough reason to be scared? Though his mother demanded, 'Get on a train and come home, son,' Ragesh knew that he was in no physical condition to travel that long a distance.

Looking at the blood report, Dr Samuel said, 'You'll have to be admitted. Has anyone come with you?' Ragesh, who lived the life of a bachelor in the city, could not think of a caretaker even in his dreams. He shook his head. 'That's okay. We'll admit you. The important thing is to recover. I'll get you someone to take care of the basics,' the doctor reassured him.

In the evening, a girl came with a loaf of bread and a bag of apples. 'Dr Samuel asked me to drop in. Let me know if you need anything.' She brought tea for him. She gave him a cold compress. She cut apples for him. She covered him with a blanket when he shivered. Ragesh stared at her in disbelief. What he needed at that point in time was the presence of a guardian angel like her. When she got up to leave after spending the visiting time of three hours with him, she gave him her phone number and reiterated that he should call if he needed anything. He apologized for the inconvenience caused and thanked her for all the help. She said humbly that formalities were not required, that what she was doing was part of her duty and responsibility. Who's she? Who's this Dr John Samuel? Why are they so kind to me? Ragesh wondered as he lay in the hospital room.

The next day, she did not come alone. Two people came along with her. Pastor Sam Philip and Brother Aruldas. They brought oranges and gruel for the night. They prayed for him for a long time in the name of Christ. Not just that day, she visited him every evening for the six days that he was in the hospital. She scolded him for not eating the apples. Pastor Philip came. Prayed. Brother Aruldas came. He gave him a brochure. Its headline read, 'This very night, your life will be demanded from you.' Everyone reminded him that he should not hesitate to call them if he needed anything, whatever it be. It was for the first time that Ragesh experienced that kind of care and attention from absolute strangers. That too, at a point in time in his life when he needed it the most. He was enveloped by their love. He decided that he would never lose this.

The Good Samaritan was Rithu. A few days after he recovered, Ragesh went to meet her with a big cake. There was an envelope full of money hidden in his pocket. He ended up being totally embarrassed at the meeting. It was when he came to know that she was the project officer at a reputed MNC that the first shade of embarrassment set in. No matter how hard he tried, he could not conceal it. He had thought that she was from a poor family, working overtime by taking care of 'orphans' like him. He had taken the money with him to reward her. He was honest and candid enough to share this truth with her. She had a good laugh. 'Our wages are paid by our Father in Heaven. We don't desire anything else.' She spoke of the fellowship. Of their coming together. Of their philosophy. Of their charities. She then invited him to experience the same purity and goodness. There was no way Ragesh could have rejected that invitation. Pastor Philip later explained it theologically, 'Yes, Calvinism says that one cannot reject the call of God.' Rithu never shared with Ragesh that getting him to accept the invitation was a task she had been entrusted with by Dr John Samuel.

29

Ragesh went back to that flat long after he recovered from his illness and the embarrassment of meeting Rithu with the gift. Reshma called Ragesh one day and said, 'I want to see the room once again, the room from where he slipped quietly into death, dreaming about me.' 'We'll go,' said Ragesh and invited Rithu, who had by then become his friend, to come along. Since the police had locked and sealed the flat as part of the investigation, Ragesh had been staying with a friend in Mayur Vihar after he came back from Chennai. Others in the flat had also moved to other places. It was after many days that the police closed the investigation and returned the key.

When they opened Kiran's room, the three of them stood stunned. Like a madman, he had covered all the four walls of the room with *Reshma, Reshma, Reshma, Reshma*, in different forms, shapes, sizes and colours. It would have taken him months, perhaps, to write all that. The three photographs of Reshma that he loved were put up in the room. Of her sitting in a pedal boat in a lake, of her standing before a tiger in a zoo, of her standing lazily after getting up in the morning. More than the photographs themselves, it was where they had been stuck that was revealing. They were on the ceiling above the bed. No matter how you lay on the bed, you could see her. That Kiran was this madly in love with her was a reality that even Reshma realized only then.

That night too, Kiran had sat speaking passionately to Reshma. It was all about getting her back into his life. But Reshma, stubborn as she was, rejected all this lightly. 'Reshma, after having made all the decisions and preparations, it was heartbreaking to speak to you as usual and beg for your love. I really want to live. I want to love. But your rejection proves that I am not fit for this world. When I leave this beautiful earth, if I feel sad about losing anyone, it will be only you. I am sorry.' This was the note that Kiran left behind before heading towards the winter of death. And the way that he chose to do it was extraordinary and intelligent.

He walked into the slumber of death by getting into a plastic bag and filling it with helium gas. The most painless way to die. Fall asleep in the arms of death. Ragesh wondered how much he would have researched and prepared before choosing that particular way to die. He would have also worked meticulously to source the helium cylinder, tubes and a bag that would not leak.

Ragesh left for his hometown the day Kiran decided to take his own life. Kiran had sent a message to Nikhil saying that there would be news waiting for him tomorrow. The police found a note from the room which said, 'If I don't succeed and if I slip into a coma, Nikhil, you should not torture me further by keeping me in the hospital. Subject me to mercy killing. This is the last request of your best friend.'

'Why did you leave the room in a huff that day? Why did you reject his apology and his love? What was it that made you hate him so much?' Ragesh asked Reshma on their way back. But her reply to all three questions was silence. That was the last time they met. He later heard that Reshma had moved to some other city like Nikhil had. Not everyone can raise their eyes to the sun. Or face it with the same intensity of love.

30

Though Ragesh and Rithu did quite a bit of research into this, they too could not come up with any satisfactory answer. However, while he was packing up to shift to another flat, Ragesh found a file in Kiran's room. He understood from it that, for some reason or the other, Kiran was really into tracking the notorious Anni Dewani murder case.

The prominent industrialist Shrien Dewani and his wife Anni Dewani had gone to South Africa for their honeymoon. While travelling through the crime-infested township of Gugulethu, two unidentified assailants attacked their car and murdered Anni, who was a Swedish model. The prosecution argued that Shrien himself had paid the driver Zola Tongo and orchestrated the murder. From the time of the murder to the time of the verdict, Kiran had tracked every argument, counterargument, accusations and the progress of the investigation across four years and gathered all the news clippings in the file. Ragesh inspected the clippings one by one. The South African court had absolved Shrien of all charges. There was not enough evidence to prove that the gay Shrien had orchestrated the murder to rid himself of his wife.

The contradictions in the statements resulted in the court also rejecting the driver Zola Tongo's confession. Ragesh and Rithu could not figure out why Kiran was so interested in this case. But they noticed that Kiran had underlined one statement given by Shrien. It was the fact that Shrien, who argued that he did not orchestrate the murder, did concede to the fact that he was a homosexual in court.

Beyond that, Ragesh and Rithu did not investigate Kiran's death any further. This sprung from the feeling that they really did not want to reach unnecessary conclusions about anything. The net outcome of the investigation was that Ragesh became a part of the fellowship and started attending the prayer group sessions regularly. Deep down, Rithu was relieved that she had brought in her quota of people.

31

Sandhya never had the habit of reading the newspaper. It was perhaps the residual outcome of her feeling that there was nothing to be gained by knowing the affairs of the world. Just the opposite of her father. He would not put down the paper in the morning without having read every single word. By evening, he would probably have read it thrice over. If she needed to know something urgently, Sandhya would watch the news on TV. Then she would instantly feel angry and change the channel. But the Sandhya who hated the news got recompense when she joined the fellowship. She was asked to read at least three regional newspapers every day. She could not refuse to do this since it was Pastor Sam Philip who, in the middle of a prayer meeting during her initial days at the fellowship, had said, 'Sandhya, the one on whom the light of salvation shines, your saviour entrusts you with a task for which you will have to find time every day.' The purpose of reading the newspaper was not to foster social awareness or get political information. The fellowship had a very specific purpose. It was to find accident victims, people who needed help and those who were alone, so that they could be reached out to in time.

While the newspapers were Sandhya's responsibility, Ragesh was in charge of social media like Facebook, and Rithu was entrusted with online magazines. This was how work was divided. 'We should not lose even one person who might come into God's fold. For that you should stay alert every single day. Your responsibility is only to find the person. Leave the rest to us.' It was not just for their group — every group was entrusted with specific responsibilities by the fellowship. 'If we don't do our job, there are a hundred other fellowships out there that enthusiastically will. We need to be more alert. It is everyone's duty to grow the fellowship. Don't see this as the responsibility of just Pastor Shanu and myself.'

In the beginning, Sandhya earnestly pursued all this. Even though it was a job that she did not quite like, she did what she was asked to and reported relevant news on time to the fellowship. And then there was office, school, divorce proceedings. Her daily routine was disrupted. It was then that she became friends with Midhun. For someone who was mad about reading, reading three newspapers in the morning was not difficult. He had the opportunity to do that in Jithin Das's office as well. It was that closeness, that reading, that enthusiasm which brought Midhun into the fellowship. The promise of a job in an MNC came later.

32

'Your God grants you everything that you ask for. Ask for what you want when you pray. If you want a car, do not just pray for a car, pray for a car that has the colour you prefer. God will never be a Scrooge.' These were the words that Pastor Sam Philip repeated all through in his speeches and briefings. He would look into every person's eyes and ask, 'Do you doubt this? For those who do, I stand before you as a witness. I landed in this city with hardly three rupees in my pocket. There is no door that I have not knocked at for a job. No street that I have not wandered in search of a place to sleep. I've had to beg for a meal from strangers. I failed miserably. Death was the last door in front of me. I decided on that, one night. I am not made for this world, the world does not need me. This has to end. It was halfway on my journey to end all this that God caught me. Like he caught Peter on the Appian Way. Like he caught Paul on the path to Jerusalem. "Come with me, I will give you everything you need," he said to me in the half-lit lane. Praise the Lord. Hallelujah! That night, I miraculously ended up in front of Pastor Cohen. He must have wondered who it was that was knocking on the door in the wee hours of the night. "Who is it? What do you want?" he asked. "It's me. I need to see God," I replied. He opened the door without any hesitation. I told him about what I had gone through. I spoke of the miracle that had led me to the door of Pastor Cohen whom I had not even heard of until then. He did not utter a word. Much later, he told to me that he had stayed awake that night because he had had a revelation about how someone would come in search of him – that night, he poured water on my head and lifted me up to the path of God. Praise the Lord. Hallelujah! And my dear brothers and sisters, I've never had to look back. God ensured that I never had to subjugate myself to anyone. I never had to beg for a meal from then on. God gave me everything I asked for – often multifold. Ask for what you need. Ask for how much you need. God is the one who gives if you ask Him. If this is what someone weak like me could achieve, so can you. All you need is unshakeable faith. This fellowship will open your door to God. Praise the Lord. Hallelujah! Hallelujah!'

Everyone knew that there was not a grain of falsehood in what Pastor Philip said. At least about his own life. His growth over ten years was amazing. He was an example of God nurturing someone right in front of your eyes. It was the kind of growth that was not possible even for business tycoons or smugglers. The person who had come with nothing was today living in the most plush apartment in the city. Cruising in a four-wheel drive. With followers across the country. Evangelism gatherings in Delhi today, Pune tomorrow, Bangalore the day after and Imphal next. Two or three miracles wherever he goes to care for the sick. Vitiligo gets cured. People with kidney problems get cured. The bedridden get up and dance. The spirits that possess the mad leave.

Apart from such public service, Pastor Philip also prayed at the homes of certain gentlemen who could not come out into the open and state what they wanted. He had several amazing skills – black magic in the name of God, exorcizing spirits, removing obstacles. 'If there is a God, there is a Devil. If God is worshipped, so is the Devil. We need to approach it that way.' That is how he justified himself. Everyone was certain that it was to show God's greatness to the world that Pastor Sam Philip was rescued from the hellhole of death. The pastor visited Rithu's neighbour's house in Goa frequently for such a secret purpose. It was through this neighbour that the pastor met Rithu, who was staying alone in Delhi, and brought her into the fold of the fellowship. Even though Kurian Sir and Mamma Lally were cynical about such practices, Rithu was, from the beginning, attracted to such paranormal powers. She had experimented with everything, ranging from palmistry to the Ouija board, and had come to believe in a few. It was then that someone who could perform miracles in front of people's eyes invited her to experience the greatness of God. She did not need any other reason to join the fellowship.

33

Rithu had seen many people who change ministries, give up ornaments, dress modestly, refrain from participating in certain rituals and stay away from celebrations and festivities. This was her only worry when she joined the fellowship. Will she have to wear white and live like a widow? Will she have to give up on the few relationships that she had until now? She did not want to give up on celebrating life in any way.

'Who said all that?' Pastor Philip reassured her personally. 'There are no such old-fashioned practices in our fellowship. God has sent us to this world to celebrate life. The Bible states that clearly in Malachi 3:10 – "I will throw open the floodgates of heaven and pour out so much blessing that there will not be room enough to store it." What else does the Parable of the Talents tell us? Haven't you read that yourself? As is said in John 10:10, "the thief comes only to steal and kill and destroy; I have come that they may have life, and have it to the full". And in the letter of Paul to the Philippians, wherein he says, "And my God will meet all your needs according to the riches of his glory in Christ Jesus"; and in the words of John, "I wish above all things that thou mayest prosper and be in health, even as thy soul prospereth". We humans own the earth and everything in it. Everything here has been created for us. I will show you a God who does not say give up everything for me, but a God who says everything has been created for you.'

That was not the only thing that attracted Rithu to the fellowship. She had always found the church of Kurian Sir and Mamma Lally boring. The same rituals as far back as she could remember. The same prayers. The same songs. Even the same beat and intonation of the priest's sermon. The very mention of church made Rithu wilt with boredom. 'Aren't you lonely in this city? Why don't you come and meet the people in our fellowship one day? If you get anything new from it, you can visit us again.' Though she accepted this invitation from Pastor Sam Philip with a twinge of scepticism, she returned from the first meeting as though she had stumbled upon an entirely new source of energy. Prayers that were based on music – not monotonous and boring, but full of energy and rhythm like the music in the dance bars of Goa. Ones that increased your heartbeat. Ones that electrified your nerves. Dance steps that matched. Making everyone want to dance. Loud shouts. Praise. Testimonials. Clapping. Laughter. Rithu realized that in addition to group prayers, sermons and silent prayers with a sari draped around the head, there was yet another way to reach out to God. A way that she had always wanted. Those were the days when she realized that she could fly with God on one wing and with a sense of joie de vivre on the other. What was wrong with that? Silence and tears were not the only two ways to know God. Haven't we seen people who praised God with drums and music? Doesn't the Bible advise us to give thanks using the harp, praise with the veena that has ten strings and celebrate with percussion? This is the way to God that I was searching for. A God whom I can ask for everything I want. A God who will let me walk the path I like. A God who teaches that I don't have to give up anything. The God of song. The God of joy. The God of celebration and prosperity.

34

S andhya's problem in the beginning was the volume at which the prayers and sermons took place. She liked music. She liked dance. She even liked sitting and listening to verses from the Bible. All at low volume levels and slow tempos. There was a time when even the blaring horns in the city were a problem for Sandhya, who was born and brought up in a remote village in Himachal Pradesh. Everyday exposure to these sounds helped her acclimatize to a certain extent. It was her lawyer who introduced her to the fellowship while her divorce proceedings were underway. He was a follower of Pastor Sam Philip. She desperately wanted an escape from loneliness, boredom and the tiredness of her heart. She tried watching movies. She tried spending hours on end in shopping malls. She went to see plays and museums. Nothing captivated her. Which is why she decided to experiment with the fellowship when her lawyer spoke to her about it.

The fellowship was good medicine for Sandhya. But the loud music, the growls of the guitar, the drumbeats that made the heart pound, the terrible sounds that Pastor Sam Philip made in between prayers, especially between prayers of healing – every time she returned after the service in the fellowship, she would say that she'd never attend meetings again because she could not tolerate the cacophony and the noise levels. Not only that, apart from singing and dancing in the bathroom and the bedroom, she was hesitant to sing or dance in public. She had an inherent rural reluctance to do so – even if it was for God. But slowly, her shell started cracking. First the rhythm conquered her heart. Then she started singing. Dancing. And then the body took over. She started clapping her hands. She experienced a new vigour that she could not fathom. This was her escape from the terrible loneliness and grief as she waited for her divorce. Soon, the 'noise' became exhilarating. Drowning in it became intoxicating.

Sandhya happily became a full-fledged member of the fellowship. It was never an innocent religious conversion for her. It was the conversion of her life.

PART SIX | *Pune*

35

'Was the vehicle that hit Midhun identified?' This question, which landed as a message from an unknown number, woke Rithu up one morning. She was in Pune for a three-week skill-upgradation programme. Rithu sat transfixed for a long while after reading the question. And then she asked in response, 'Why, do you know?' 'No. But looking into it might give you many answers' was the reply she got. That made her really mad. She called that number in vain. She tried calling that number during all the intervals in the programme that day. But not once was the number reachable. She decided that someone was just pulling a fast one on her.

In spite of that, she called Sandhya and Ragesh to ask the same question without mentioning anything about the message that she had received that morning.

'Is it possible in our Delhi? How many such vehicles hit people and just drive away – has anyone found out to whom these vehicles belong? The fate of this will also be the same,' Ragesh said in anger.

'But it is no longer like in the past. The city is full of cameras – so the chances of identifying the vehicle are higher. Especially if the police set their mind to it,' Rithu said.

'For many days, this thought has been on my mind every night before I go to sleep. But nothing seems to work here. So I concluded helplessly that Midhun was just another ordinary guy with no contact or influence where it mattered,' said Sandhya.

They decided that the issue should be raised with Pastor Philip to find out if they could get some lead or the other.

'What did you think? That I had forgotten all that? You might have just lost a friend. But what the fellowship lost was a trusted brother. Dr Samuel and I have been on this since day one. The police camera recorded a car that shot by like an arrow at the time of the accident. They are trying hard to trace that car,' the pastor said, when Sandhya met him the next day. 'Even for the insurance money to be released, the vehicle has to be identified. Money is not a substitute for anything. But it will be a small relief for his family. This is another reason why we are pursuing the investigation.'

When Sandhya heard that, she hung her head in shame and guilt. Not just in front of the pastor who always walked one step ahead of them, but also in front of Midhun's mother whom she had not called even once after they had left – she had been too caught up in her own grief to even think about them. She called Midhun's mother that evening, prepared to listen to anything that she might have to say. 'Why did you not call even once?' Midhun's mother scolded Sandhya.

She abused a few people. She cursed the God who had left them alone in the world. Sandhya did not quite comprehend the many things she said. But she understood that Pastor Philip was the only person who had kept in touch with Midhun's parents, and also that he had given them a large sum of money from the fellowship.

When Sandhya told her all this, the seed of doubt that had been planted in Rithu's mind by the unknown person's message wilted. But two days later, in an unexpected moment, she received another message from the same number: 'Your vehicle is running on the wrong track. To get to the right track, you need to travel quite a distance in another direction.' Rithu got really angry. She replied: 'I am not interested in hide-and-seek games like the ones in third-rate detective novels. If you have something to say, meet me in person.'

'The meeting can happen. But I will not come – another person will meet you. My role is just to clear the way for him' was the response. There were no further messages from that number.

Rithu was suddenly scared. She felt that she was not safe in Pune. The thought that somebody was following her became stronger. She even mentioned this fear vaguely to Ragesh when they spoke on the phone. But he did not pay any heed to it. However, from that day onwards, she took care not to be really alone and to not go out at odd hours. She felt like seeing Kurian Sir and Mamma Lally. She even sent an email to the office asking if she could take leave after the programme in Pune. Her manager reprimanded her, 'You have not been in office for three weeks and you want to take leave before you even come back to work? You cannot take any more leaves for a year. Come straight to Delhi!' That night, unable to sleep, Rithu called Pastor Philip. She cried and said that someone was following her, that she was feeling very scared in this city. Over the phone, the pastor said a prayer for her. He also gave her the number of a fellowship in the city. He instructed her to join them in prayer every day until the end of the course. She felt relieved that she might get to meet like-minded people in this city. From the next day onwards, Rithu started going to the fellowship every evening. It was here that she unexpectedly met a girl called Pretty John.

36

Pretty's house was on the outskirts of Kochi. Her father was with the air force. After he retired, he took a test and got a job at the port. Her mother was an officer in a private bank. Both of them belonged to respected families from the hill town of Ranni. Though they had inherited large landholdings there, they settled down in Kochi because of the job Pretty's father had taken up. Their relatives were still in Ranni. This contented family of Papa, Mamma, Pretty and her sister lived the typical happy city life, isolated and insulated from everyone. Their social engagements were limited to going to the church – one worthy of the Christian aristocracy of Ranni – spending the evenings at the club, visiting the shopping mall once a week and going to the movies at the end of the month. Neither they nor society seemed to expect more.

This river of life was flowing happily and peacefully through the city of Kochi until the day Pretty's sister eloped with a Nair boy she had met on Facebook. Though they rescued her on the thirteenth day from her friend's apartment in Bangalore, that was more than enough for the aristocratic Christian family from Ranni to lose face. They lost their stature in the community they lived in and became the butt of jokes. Mamma stopped going to the church. Papa stopped going to the club and started having his drink at home. Her sister was kept under house arrest. But Pretty went on with her life unaffected, either because of her inherent ignorance or her new-gen bravery.

Silence, like death, permeated the house – and it was this house that Pastor Sam Philip visited one day. He came with a long-lost friend of Papa. Even though Papa and Mamma managed to hold the fort with a certain amount of indifference, Papa eventually broke down and wept in front of Pastor Philip. The pastor prayed for them. He had a vision during the prayer. A vision of fat calves swallowing thin calves. 'One chapter of life ends here. A new chapter opens in your life from tomorrow. That will be one of auspiciousness. One of prosperity. One of joy. Our living God wishes to come into your midst to work his miracles. Believe my words only if all your sorrows vanish; only if the living God solves all the problems in your life.' It was after giving such a guarantee that Pastor Philip left Pretty's house.

Pastor Sam Philip was the messiah of love who walked in where no one else had. From the next week onwards, Pretty's parents started going for the service held by a fellowship in Vyttila. The pastor visited them whenever he was in Kochi. But this was not how the pastor won over the love and trust of that family. He brought an alliance for Pretty's sister from Nagpur, thereby washing away the blot on the family caused by her elopement with the Nair boy.

From then onwards, Mamma became a full-fledged member of the fellowship and Papa became a donor who would contribute generously for any cause.

'God restored the honour I had lost. Now all that I earn will be his.' That was Papa's rationale.

'Contribute to charity without holding back. He will give it back to you tenfold.' The pastor encouraged him thus.

Thereon, whenever the pastor was in the city, he joined the family for dinner. And whenever that happened, Mamma would specially get pearlspot from Alleppey, mussels from Thalassery, tapioca from Kanjirappally, beef from Chalakudy, country chicken from Perumbavoor and bananas from Palakkad. And she would send jackfruit chips, beef pickle, dried tapioca and chutney powder for the pastor's wife Susan, through him. Even when it came to Pretty's college admission, Papa did not have to search for anyone else. Though the forty lakhs that came in from the sale of Mamma's share of the property in Ranni had to be given, Pastor Philip secured a BDS (Bachelor of Dental Surgery) admission for Pretty in an autonomous college in Coimbatore. Later, when a priest came from the church to visit, Papa dismissed him summarily, calling priests 'white gowns that go a feasting and a begging.' That was, in a way, a declaration that his relationship with the church was over forever. Though Pretty was not too keen on letting go of the church, this was totally ignored by everyone at home. Finally, after Pretty completed her degree, it was Pastor Philip who took her to Pune, and found a job as well as an accommodation for her.

All of a sudden, Pretty went silent when she realized that she had told the story of her whole life. And then she asked Rithu a question that had nothing to do with all this: 'Did you succeed in identifying the vehicle that knocked Midhun down and sped away?'

37

'Was it you who sent me the message?' Rithu asked Pretty without batting an eyelid.

'What message?' asked Pretty, eyebrows raised.

'Leave it. I was just making a wild guess,' Rithu replied, trying to make light of it.

But Pretty was not willing to let go. 'I am curious, naturally. What message were you talking about?'

Rithu told her in detail about the messages she had received. For a full minute, Pretty sat staring at Rithu. There was more mystery on her face than Rithu could fathom. She then took her mobile out and showed Rithu a message. It was the same one that Rithu had received. And from the same number.

'It's not only this, Rithu. I got another message saying that, for the time being, I should discuss this issue only with you.' Pretty showed that message to Rithu too.

'Someone is either trying to fool us or there is something dark hiding behind this question,' said Rithu. 'But what I don't understand is, why us? Two people who are from far-flung cities. Not only that, Midhun was closest to Sandhya – she is the one who used to think of and worry about him the most.

But she has not got this message. I'm really confused. Why, Pretty? Why are Ragesh and Sandhya, my close friends, left out of this? Why was this not sent to anyone in Delhi but only to you in Pune?'

'I have no clue, Rithu. I have been trying to contact you ever since I got this message.'

'Let this be just between the two of us for now. I will use my contacts to investigate this. We'll decide what to do after that.'

It was on that note of relief that they parted. But there was no relief for Rithu that night. She debated whether she should share this with Ragesh and Sandhya. She was unable to make up her mind. She had mentioned this to Ragesh earlier. But he hadn't really paid any heed to it. That was what made her anxious. And the fact that she did not know how Sandhya would react to all this.

When doubt really started gnawing at her, she opened the Bible like she always did to find out what God would tell her.

It was Mathai 9:30 that she saw. 'Then their eyes were opened, and they could see! Jesus sternly warned them, "Don't tell anyone about this."' Rithu felt that the words had been written just for her. And that they had been waiting for her all these years. This put an end to her doubt. Having decided that nobody else needed to know of this now, she slept peacefully.

The very next day, with the help of a friend who was an IT professional, Rithu started the process of tracing the owner of that mobile number. It was not a difficult task. Her friend gave her the answer in three hours. The connection was in the name of Jyothi Krishna Munde, a farmer in Jharkhand. It did not need anything beyond Rithu's Goan intelligence to figure out that it was a fake number obtained using the identity of Jyothi Krishna Munde.

'It is not to whom it belongs, but the reason why he chose to send this message to strangers like us that we should find out,' said Pretty.

38

The next day, there was a charity sale organized by the Pune fellowship. This was an annual event. The homemakers in the fellowship would make pickle, banana chips and payasam and put them up for sale. It was mandatory for every member to bring something. Since most people did not have time to cook or create, they would buy stuff from shops based on what they could afford and their standing in the society. From bed sheets to gold coins, air conditioners to silk saris, casseroles to carpets.

All these items would be auctioned in the evening. Since it was for charity, people would bid without being parsimonious. Slowly, it would turn into a heated, obstinate competition. Something worth a thousand rupees would get auctioned for ten thousand. Members of the fellowship from all over the country would come to Pune just to participate in this auction.

At times, Rithu felt a tad uncomfortable with this performance. True, it was for charity. But what was disturbing was that this competitive bidding seemed to be a race to establish that 'I am in no way inferior to you'. Ragesh would never agree with this. 'These are the ways in which we can bring out the money certain people hoard in order to serve other people. This is a smart way of getting fifty from the guy who wants to give just five. If you are not interested, just sit there quietly and then leave.' Though she had no one to share it with, in her mind Rithu kept debating whether people should be made to contribute to a cause by triggering their competitive spirit or by awakening the goodness in them. She was sure that if she shared this thought with anyone, she would be misunderstood.

This thought was much stronger while participating in the sale hosted by the fellowship in another city. Her mind resisted every minute of it. She kept muttering to herself, 'This is not right, this is not right…' At one point, Pretty seemed to have understood Rithu's state of mind. She got Rithu to step out with her. They ordered tea from a dhaba nearby.

'I could sense that you were not able to bear it any more, Rithu. I too was looking for an opportunity to step out. Though my parents kept insisting, it is actually because I've always had an inbuilt resistance to priesthood and its theatrics that I became part of the fellowship. What I expected was pure love for Christ and a way of life founded on that. To be honest, Rithu, I have not seen even an iota of that here until now. It is what is wrong about priesthood that one sees here, manifested many times over. So what difference is this fellowship going to make? What change will it bring about?'

Rithu remained silent for a while. And then she said, 'No. It's not like that. Our worship, prayers, songs, the pastor's visions, his ability to cure the sick – all of these make a difference. I believe in this and I enjoy the process.' She said these words in a muted tone, almost as though she were trying to convince herself.

'Who is this person you are talking about?' Pretty asked a bit harshly. 'Your voice will always betray you when you say things that you are really not convinced about. Your voice just betrayed you.'

'You really have not told me something, have you?' Rithu asked, with a mixture of fear and expectation on her face.

'Yes. But I don't know how prepared you are to listen to it. In fact, I have been trying to gauge that over the last couple of days.'

'Whatever it is, say it. I will go insane if I don't know what it is.'

Pretty stepped out of the dhaba along with Rithu. They walked a while through the crowded streets.

'Haven't you heard that what we see and what we believe in need not always be right? This is applicable to our fellowship as well. I can't say this to anyone outside the fellowship. And if I say this to people within, they will not believe me either. That is the bind that faith puts you in. The people behind all this know it well. Once you are in, you can never extricate yourself. That is their strength. But if I don't say it, I will suffocate and die. My family and I are in a crisis. I had told you all about why and how we joined the fellowship. By then, everyone in the family trusted Pastor Philip implicitly. I saw that trust helping him establish a new authority over my family. Papa surrendered completely to the pastor. And the pastor became the Rasputin who controls everything in the family. That's how Papa's money flows out. That's okay. But Mamma … I saw it with my own eyes one day. That's why he comes home to sleep at night. From what I understand, he is not only taking advantage of their trust but threatening them as well. Mamma knows that a word from the pastor is all it will take to end the future of her happily married elder daughter settled in Nagpur. My sister's in-laws are greater believers than us. For long they had problems selling their five hundred acres of land in Nasik, thanks to a few politicians and local goondas. It was Pastor Philip who solved the problem and sold the land effortlessly. With that, the pastor's words came to be adored more by that family than the words of the Bible. But to whom can I tell all this, Rithu? Even if I do, who will believe me? I was living with all this bottled up inside me. Until I got that message. It increased my fear. I think the links in this chain go far beyond what I had thought. Do you have the courage to stand with me, Rithu? If so, we can travel a bit in search of the truth behind that message.'

Rithu did not respond. She walked with Pretty for a while without making eye contact. And then she got into a bus which stopped near them and went away without saying a word.

PART SEVEN | *Delhi*

39

Rithu's fear led her to Sandhya's apartment. Meanwhile, she called Ragesh and asked him if he could join them. She was hoping that his presence would give her the energy she needed. But he, the classic lover, slipped away like the proverbial eel, saying light-heartedly that instead of him coming all the way to Sandhya's apartment, they could speak sometime over the phone. That was the day Rithu had returned to Delhi from Pune after completing her course. She spent the rest of the evening in Sandhya's apartment. She played with Sandhya's daughter Aparna, who was back from boarding school for the holidays. She rambled for a while about Uncle Carlos to Sandhya, and recalled that the first time she had read the words 'Himachal Pradesh' was at the railway station – on the board of the HPMC store selling apple juice, which she used to drool over. And then she narrated a story that she had heard.

A beautiful girl used to visit the cemetery every day to pray at the grave of her lover. Over time, the caretaker of the cemetery fell in love with her. But she rejected his love, saying that she would never be able to fall in love with anyone again. One day, while they were talking, the body of a dead man the caretaker was entrusted with was stolen. He was certain that the king would kill him. 'All you need is a dead body to show – you can take my man instead,' she said to him kindly.

'What exactly are you trying to tell me, Rithu?' asked a slightly incensed Sandhya. 'What is the lifespan of love?' asked Rithu in return. Sandhya told Rithu not to work her up into a tizzy and allow her to crawl back to life, which, right now, kept defeating her every step of the way. She said that the fellowship, the prayer group and charity work were the things that gave her some relief. All the while, everything that Pretty had said kept churning in Rithu's mind. Many a time, she was on the verge of saying it out loud. Suddenly, she was reminded of the Biblical verse that appeared for her. 'Jesus sternly warned them, "Don't tell anyone about this."'

'Sorry, I wasn't trying to say anything. It just felt as if Midhun was knocking at the door,' said Rithu and left the apartment rejecting Sandhya's offer to drop her back home on the scooty.

She called Pretty the next day. 'What's your plan, Pretty?'

'I don't have a clear plan. Just a hunch – that message was not an innocent one. It's from someone who is afraid to come out into the open. He is gauging our courage. If we start moving on this, I think he will too.'

'Hmm, hmm.' Rithu did not say anything. That was enough. Her observation was too precise to counter.

'So where do we start?' she asked.

'From Midhun's deathbed,' said Pretty. 'I know a girl who works in the ICU of that hospital. I will connect the two of you. Will you go see her?'

Rithu had no qualms about doing that. They met in the veranda of Medical Trust on the day both of them could take time off. The nurse was waiting for Rithu as Pretty had said she would. The name of this nurse who sported gold streaked, navy-cut hair was Jane. 'Just finished my duty. I'm really hungry,' she said, even before she introduced herself. They walked on Moti Marg to the Subway in the lane opposite Sri Venkateswara College and ordered a six-inch-long oven-roasted chicken sub and a medium cola. When four inches of that sandwich had gone in, Jane asked, 'Why did you want to meet me?'

'We need your help,' Rithu said.

'That much I got. If not, there is no reason why you should buy an American sandwich for a person like me. Tell me what it's all about.'

Rithu liked her open approach. That would make it easy to get right to the heart of the matter.

'Midhun, a patient who died in your hospital recently, was a very good friend of ours. When he was admitted, he did not have any injury on his body that could have resulted in death. So could you tell me what really happened in the hospital?'

'Oh, I see. So you have in-depth knowledge of anatomy. Have you read anywhere that only a person with external wounds can die?'

'That is not it, Jane. We, his friends, were there with him right from the time he was admitted. The doctors there were also close to us. There was no lack of attention. In spite of that, how on earth did he…? This is not for anything other than coming to terms with what happened and trying to find some peace of mind.'

'If it is peace of mind you want, he had enough bleeding to cause death. That could not be controlled. I would say that it was the will of God ... But my conscience does not allow me to grant you peace of mind by offering you this explanation and walking away,' said Jane, without any emotion.

'What does that mean?' Rithu's heart was pounding.

'You have the intelligence to figure it out. The rules of the hospital forbid me from saying any more. I also need to protect the interests of the people who pay me. I said this much only because Pretty told me a thousand times that I could trust you. She was my classmate for years. I hope my trust in her will not prove to be unfounded.'

'Yes. You can trust me completely,' Rithu said. After that, to every question she asked, Jane had only one reply, 'Everything is there in what I have already told you.'

40

'Friendship comes with a privilege – one can spout utter nonsense and then get the other person to respect that nonsense.' This was the message she got from Ragesh when she told him about her conversation with Jane. Rithu was taken aback. 'A good lover is a good listener. When you dismiss what I say as nonsense, I feel that we are diminishing our relationship,' she replied.

'No, Rithu. We are not diminishing anything. I decided that you are mine long ago. On my next trip, I will tell Appa that I have found my saviour. And tell Amma that I have found my girl. They will not accept either. All hell will break loose. That might even be my last trip to Chennai. Before that, I need to settle down in Delhi. Must buy a flat. And a car. I want to bring you to a place that has everything. You should not want for anything. I don't want Kurian Sir reprimanding you for having come away with me. I'm running around to make all this happen – and I want nothing else to get in the way. I think that you should not poke your nose into things unnecessarily. Just know that God calls people who are dear to him quickly. How he does this will never be known to us.

If not, why Midhun? Couldn't it have been you or me or someone else? There was a reason behind God's choice.'

'Hmm. You have decided everything, haven't you? Including my likes and dislikes. But you don't have to run around to make anything happen for me. I have not taken any decision about my future. It is not mandatory that every friendship has to end in marriage.'

This reply from Rithu brought that conversation to an abrupt end. Ragesh set everything aside and came over to see her the next day. 'Men will put aside anything if they feel that they are going to lose something, right?' Rithu teased him. Ragesh, who was expecting a battle, was pleasantly surprised at her light-heartedness.

'I'm not the kind of girl you are used to seeing. I have my own way of living life – and this is applicable to trust, love and marriage. So let's walk alone for a while. And then, if both of us feel that we want the relationship, we'll think about walking together and then, marriage.'

There was no way to counter Rithu's resolve. They finished their coffee in silence and parted. Before speeding off on her scooty from the parking lot, she said, 'Please tell Sandhya that I will not be there for home-prayer any more.'

Rithu kept driving through the never-ending streets of Delhi for a long time that day. Almost as though she was trying to prove that a girl could speed through the streets of Delhi without the support of God and men. Finally, when she stopped, she felt a strange self-confidence. And it was this self-confidence that made her call Jane again.

'Oh Rithu! You have not let go of this until now? Pretty also called me. Something has happened to you people. Keep your doubts in your head. Don't share them with anyone in the fellowship. I would like to keep my job here for a while,' she said, half seriously and half in jest.

'No. Don't worry. I will not share what's on my mind with anyone. I need to meet you once more.'

'If you take me to Subway, I'll meet you as many times as you want. But if you expect any new information, it will be a loss for you!'

'What is life if we just chase profits all the time, Jane?

'Ah! Philosophy! Okay, I will come.'

That is how they met a second time. Rithu did not ask anything about Midhun that day on purpose. All she asked was how Jane became a part of the fellowship.

'It was when we were struggling to cope with the fact that even after the third round of chemotherapy my mother was not free of cancer, that a pastor from our home town came to visit us along with my father. The pastor succeeded in making us believe that our lack of belief was the real problem. That was a phase when we had tried everything in vain – from the paradise tree to the soursop and from Yunani to tribal medicine. We were willing to go to any extent to save her – and we fell for that temptation … What are you thinking? That you have heard other versions of the same story?'

'No. A few words that you used – consciously or unconsciously – struck me. "Tempting" a person to believe.

I was just wondering why no one is refuting anything in spite of having the awareness to use such words.'

'It is not because of a lack of awareness, Rithu. It is because of the helplessness that sets in when you know that all doors are closed firmly. There's also shame and financial loss involved. The only option is to keep moving from one fellowship to another in an attempt to delude yourself that you are trying to escape. This is the third fellowship that I am part of. What makes me stay on here is the fact that I get the same salary as I would get in AIIMS.'

'And after that?'

'There's nothing after that, Rithu.'

'The spirituality that the fellowship provides?'

'Makes me want to laugh. Is there anything like that, Rithu? How many people in the fellowship desire salvation? Are we not first-class selfish creatures who have come together knowing that Christ is a first-class businessman?'

They parted promising each other that they would meet the next day to try out another American sandwich.

41

'I don't know if you have heard this story, Rithu. Long ago, a long, long time ago, there lived a madman in our village. One day, the Devi appeared in front of him and told him that she would grant him anything he wished for. "Wish?" he asked. "For me? I don't want anything. Just leave me alone." The Devi said, "No, I will go only after granting you a wish." The madman had elephantiasis on his left leg. "Okay if you are that insistent, just shift my elephantiasis from my left leg to my right leg." There is also another story like this. Once, when a Zen guru was soaking in the morning sun, the king appeared in front of him and told him that he would give him whatever he needed. The Zen guru told the king calmly that he did not need anything from him. "However, if you are insistent on helping me, I request you to move aside from where you are now. I was basking in the sunlight – and your shadow is blocking it." Rithu, when you say passionately that God will give you everything that you want once you are really close to Him, you need to think once in a while of the madman and the guru who did not want anything. To a man with no desire, what is the kind of God that you are going to talk about?'

It was her colleague Prakash Warrier's words that came unexpectedly to her mind as Rithu lay awake in the wee hours of the morning. He was responding to her spiel on the greatness of the fellowship and why he should be part of it. That was the time when Prakash had brought a large debt upon himself and was tied up in litigation regarding the same. 'If you can't catch a person like that, whom can you catch?' The pastor's rebuke was what gave Rithu the courage to approach Prakash Warrier. She had brushed aside the response she got then with disdain: 'If they can't find God in the midst of great adversity, they must be so lost.' She felt sorry for her colleague – he was rejecting the great luxuries that came from knowing God. But this morning, as she lay awake, she heard his response from a completely different perspective. Are there people in this world who really have nothing to ask of God? People who have no interest in what we call the comforts of life? What Christ shall I talk to them about? The fellowship had never answered that question. Every day I meet people who approach God for illnesses to be cured, for peace of mind, for more money, for more profit, for a better quality of life. Would there not be another Christ for people who are not like that? Why is it that we don't strive to find Him?

There was another reason behind the way Rithu was thinking. Kurian Sir had sent his daughter a few more chapters of his book for her to translate. After having repeatedly postponed the assignment due to work pressure, Rithu had just started on it the previous evening. She finished it in one go and emailed it as well. Rithu never had the habit of reviewing an assignment she had completed. For the same reason, many things had become a part of her day-to-day life over time – getting upset over the first set of questions that she eventually forgot to answer; getting hassled over the fact that she forgot to sign the application form after filling it up and dropping it off; standing with her head bowed before the manager who found fault with her for errors that she could have easily rectified … But that day, she had the foresight to read the material she had translated for her father from the point of view of a reader. They were the speeches made at the condolence meeting held after the burial of Pastor Alvares by Justice Antonio, Araújo Mascarenhas – Director of Agriculture, Casimiro de Sequeira – representative of the people, and Cordato de Noronha – representative of the youth. There has not been a missionary like Alvares after his time. A missionary who had to undergo tremendous hardships and torture. A missionary who was chased away from his land because he was kind to others. A missionary who was arrested based on fabricated cases. A man who went begging to feed the poor, a man who carried the sick to hospital in his own arms, a man who was paraded half naked through the streets and then shut in a dungeon – these were the statements made about him in the speeches. This was the history of a man who rejected the titles, the bungalows and the comforts that teaming up with the ruling Portuguese would have given him, and instead, chose to serve the poor and the sick. Even if one were to dismiss part of this as heightened eulogy, the intriguing fact was that it was the same people who opposed him tooth and nail who were now calling him a saint.

Why was this man, or rather, many men like him, doing the work of God without expecting anything in return? Why are they willing to give up all the comforts of life and dedicate their life to the poor? So there are people who search for and find God in a completely different way, quite different from mine. People who need God just to transfer elephantiasis from one leg to another. Or people who don't need God for even that much. There was a sudden urge from deep within Rithu to discover the God of such people. She hated herself when she thought about the list of wishes she would have presented if God had appeared in front of her as he had appeared in front of the madman.

42

They met again. Rithu and Jane. At Subway. At Starbucks. At Kulfi Ice Creams. They only had casual conversations. Both of them were careful not to bring Midhun into the picture. They spent a couple of evenings at Nehru Park. They went to Sarojini Market once. They ate momos from a street shop. They shared a Delhi joke at the expense of Jane's aunt, who told her, 'When you go to Karol Bagh, please buy a good bag for me.'

'Rithu, you need to keep in touch with her without fail. Until she is ready to divulge what she has not told us so far. "Do not excite love, do not stir it up, until the time is ripe and you're ready" – this verse in the Song of Solomon is applicable to not just love, but also secrets.' It was Pretty's words that inspired Rithu to set up meetings with Jane.

When they met that day, Rithu told Jane a story. With a prelude she did not know was a true story or not. 'Once, four hired assassins were waiting in four different spots with guns to kill the Cuban president Fidel Castro. They had plugged all the loopholes and made all the necessary preparations. As luck would have it, that day, the Latin American writer Gabriel

Garcia Márquez was also with Castro. Just because of that, the assassins did not open fire. They justified their decision saying that when a great writer like Márquez is with someone, we cannot open fire on them.'

'Behind the telling of every story, there is a purpose. But that purpose need not be understood by everyone in the same way. Beyond the fact that a writer saved a politician, what is the meaning of this story as you see it, Rithu? Especially between us?' Jane asked, patting her golden hair into place.

'Isn't it because there is someone we love in the middle that we hesitate to pull the trigger on our enemy?' Rithu asked. Jane sat silent for a while.

'I am intelligent enough to understand what you are trying to say. Very often it is not just one person in between, Rithu. It could be many people, many things. In my case, it's medical ethics, the loyalty to the place I work in, the love for my family – why, even the fear for my own life – it's all there. Even then, I will tell you what I know. If you promise me that you will never ever breathe a word of it to anyone.'

Rithu understood that the moment had come. The moment, in the words of Solomon, when love is ready. The moment, in the words of Pretty, when the mind chooses to pour itself out. Rithu did not say a word. She knew that the writer should never appear when it is time to pull the trigger.

'I was there right from the time Midhun was admitted. It is true that his bleeding was quite serious. Moving him to the ICU and then putting him on a ventilator were totally justified. The first thing that puzzled me was the fact that he was not getting enough oxygen on the ventilator. I noticed this twice or thrice during my duty. The knob on the cylinder was turned very low. I don't know if someone did it intentionally or not.'

Though she had taken a firm resolve not to let anything trigger her, Rithu could not help but jump the gun. 'What harm will this cause a patient?' she asked.

'Brain death due to lack of oxygen.'

'Are you saying, Jane, that Midhun did not die in the accident, but was actually murdered in the hospital?'

'I can't say that for sure. This is a suspicion that I have. Even if it were true, at this age, who would have held such a grudge against him?'

It took Rithu two minutes to assess all the possibilities. Finally, her wild guess was Sandhya's ex-husband. That seemed to be a possibility. He could have been taking revenge on the young man who was in a relationship with his wife. Executed in cahoots with someone in the hospital.

'We can create a story like that if we want,' said Jane. 'Everyone might believe it as well. But my mind tells me that things are not as simple as that.'

'Why?'

'I don't know if it can be connected to this. Yet I will tell you. Two days before the accident, Midhun had come to the hospital and had a conversation with Dr John Samuel.'

'What was that for?'

'I don't know that, Rithu. I was not on duty that day. It was when I went to meet the doctor to get a signature on my casual-leave application that I saw this young man there. Because I had met him at the fellowship, I asked him why he was there. He just said that he had dropped in to have a chat with the doctor. Two days later, when he was brought in after the accident, I thought of this.'

'Can you connect all these links into one chain, Jane?'

'No, Rithu. Which is why I never shared these doubts with anyone. Maybe all of this is my imagination. You are smart. And you have the ability to probe the human mind. I had taken a vow that I would never speak to you about all this no matter how hard you tried. But you got everything that you wanted from me effortlessly. So you should go ahead. Until you know enough to remove all the doubts from your mind.'

'Will you be with me in that journey, Jane?'

Jane did not reply. They sat silently for a while and then parted. Before leaving, Jane said, 'You also need to find out why Midhun was brought this far to a private hospital instead of being taken to Safdarjung, which was close to the site of the accident, or to Ram Manohar Lohia or even to AIIMS.'

PART EIGHT | *Bhopal*

43

One day, the three-year-old daughter of the famous writer Ursula K. Le Guin showed her mother a matchbox and asked her to guess what was inside. Butterfly, firefly, flower, coin, rat, puppy, elephant … a curious Ursula kept on answering. But in the end, the daughter opened the box a bit for her mother to see and said, 'Nothing. Just darkness.'

Rithu, who expected butterflies, puppies and even elephants in the box that Jane had opened, got just darkness. A darkness that was darker than the one she had known so far.

She called Pretty in Pune and shared everything.

'Do you think Jane has really told you everything?' Pretty asked.

'Yes. I don't think we will get anything more from her,' Rithu replied.

'That's not what I think, Rithu. We will be able to dig more information out of her. Keep that in mind. There is nothing wrong in suspecting Sandhya's husband. But I don't think he would have been able to influence Dr Samuel so much. Just keep that as a possibility in your mind. There is no need to waste time chasing it now.'

'That's true. That was just a hunch that I shared with Jane. Later when I thought about it, I too felt that there was nothing there. The doctor is an ardent devotee of the pastor,' Rithu responded. 'A person outside the fellowship can never influence a person inside the fellowship. That's how strong the fellowship is. At times when I hear him speak, I think that the doctor believes more in the pastor than in Christ. He keeps saying that the only reason he grew from being an ordinary physician in Apollo to the head of such a large hospital is the prayer of the pastor.'

'Not only that, at a time when it is easy to bump someone off, I don't think Sandhya's husband would pick such a convoluted route. It is Jane's parting shot that we need to focus on. What were the tests done on Midhun that day? She herself might be able to answer this question. Or she definitely will be able to introduce us to the person who can. We need to be patient until Jane is ready to do that. In this journey, Rithu, at times we should be able to walk in the dark with measured footsteps.'

Their conversation for the day ended thus.

Norman Mailer has written somewhere about the trauma a plant undergoes when it is moved from one location and replanted in another. If a plant undergoes trauma, you can imagine what it will do to human beings – Rithu was suddenly reminded of this comment made by Midhun in the early days of their friendship. Theirs was a friendship that existed separate from Sandhya. A friendship sealed by Malayalam, the language that only the two of them knew.

Though born and brought up in Goa, Rithu's strength was the Malayalam that Kurian Sir taught her on Sundays, saying that knowing more than one language was not a sin. Sandhya would sulk when she was with them, because they spoke in a language that she could not comprehend. To irk her even more, they would continue to speak in Malayalam. And Sandhya would really lose it when Ragesh too would join in with them. She would curse three generations of 'Madrasi morons' to get over her anger. Midhun would speak about the trauma of being uprooted from an absolutely rural life and being replanted in the heart of the city. Some people acclimatize to the city very quickly. But his sorrow was that he could not. During these moments, he would look frightened and sad, drained of self-confidence, like a refugee washed ashore from a wrecked boat.

'Why are you so frightened when Sandhya is here for you? When we are all here for you? When you have the love and the presence of the fellowship?' Rithu would ask angrily. Though he had been a 'seeker' in the fellowship for over six months, Midhun's response to Jesus was, 'God or man – he does not have the right to call me.' Rithu never understood what he meant by this. But she knew that it was not a meaningless rejection of God. Midhun had his own rationale for everything. He was never bothered about whether it was acceptable to anyone or not. Though she kept asking him what it meant, Midhun would always say, 'You are not old and mature enough to understand.' But when Rithu persisted, he spoke about it one day with this prelude: 'I don't know how much of this you will get, but here goes. I have tried to study Christ in every way possible. "If so, follow me" – just this statement made me realize that we will never get along well. How does Christ expect me to follow him? As a man? If yes, which of the crises that I face has he faced in his life? My temptations, my frustrations, my sexuality, my love, my problems at work, my problems at home, my emotional issues, my fears – has he faced even a single one of these in his life? How can a man who does not know my life tell me to follow him? How can we walk on the same path? On the other hand, if he is a God asking me to walk with him, shouldn't he first bless me with strength and courage that are worthy of himself? Wouldn't it be better if he makes me an equal before inviting me to walk with him? So long as he and I are two distinctly different personalities, how can he tell me to walk with him? I will not be able to, Rithu. If I should, I will have to start deceiving myself. I don't wish to live like that. I would like to be my own self as long as I live.'

Rithu had not understood much of what he had said. She had only corroborated Sandhya's theory in her mind – that one day, Midhun would become a writer or a philosopher.

44

There is an interesting story about Pastor Shanu within the fellowship. He came in to teach Hindi to Pastor Ko Hee-sung. Other than his knowledge of the Hindi language, he knew pretty much nothing about Christ then. Why, Shanu had not even heard of Christ. One day, Pastor Ko gave Shanu a piece of cake saying that it was Christmas the next day. After relishing the last crumb of the cake, Shanu asked what Christmas was all about. Christmas is the day on which Christ was born, the pastor told him calmly. 'Who is this Christ? Is he the MD of your company?' was Shanu's innocent question. From that day onwards, in return for teaching him Hindi, Pastor Ko taught Shanu everything about Christ. Shanu emerged three years later as the pastor in charge of the Hindi service in the fellowship. This was the story that Jane told Rithu when they met next, after one cancelled meeting.

'What happened that day after you promised you would come?' Rithu asked.

'I had to go to Bhopal all of a sudden. When I had just moved to Delhi, there was an Aunty Annie who did everything for me and made really tasty local food for me every weekend. She was my mother's classmate. She passed away in Bhopal. I had to go see her. It was really tiring going by the night train without reservation.'

'Oh! You should have told me. I would have come with you,' said Rithu sympathetically.

'We were really close friends in every way, though we were like mother and daughter so far as the difference in age goes. I always felt that Aunty was either reliving her youth through me or treating me like a friend from her youth. What is interesting is that, like my mother, she also became a believer very late in life. That too, after Uncle Cherian died. As someone who knew them well, I thought it was the shock of his passing that had brought Aunty into the fellowship – until she told me the real reason one day. I always keep thinking that every life is so different and so inexplicable from what we see on the outside. It was after forty-two long years of married life that Uncle Cherian passed away. "I decided to change ministries three days after he died," Aunty Annie told me later. "I was not really bothered about which ministry it was, what their beliefs were, or anything. I just wanted to ensure that after I died, I would not be buried in the same church that he was buried in. I put up with him for forty-two years. At least after my death, I don't want his presence anywhere near me. That was the only reason why I changed my ministry." Her last days were spent in Bhopal along with her younger sister. She was scared that if she stayed on in Delhi, one of her children might bury her along with her husband. I don't think anyone else knows about this,' Jane said. 'For everyone else, she continues to be a gem of a lady who sought solace in belief and the fellowship because of the sheer grief caused by her husband's passing.'

Every person has a different reason to turn to faith. That was what Rithu thought at that moment. I have a reason. Sandhya has a reason. Ragesh has a reason. Pretty and Jane have their reasons. Aunty Annie had her very own reason. Only Midhun had reasons not to turn to faith.

45

'Truth be told, I did not come here to tell you all this. It's just that, as I was speaking, the story changed,' Jane said. 'At the funeral of Aunty Annie, I met someone from Delhi. Jacob Chettan, who was Pastor Ko's driver. He was in Delhi until recently. He is now a driver in a company based in Bhopal. He heard about Aunty Annie's death and came to help; he is from her native town. But no help was required. Now every pastor has an event management group. They undertake everything from marriages to funerals and do everything that is needed. They don't need the help of any Jacob Chettan. When he heard that I am from Delhi, he came over and introduced himself. He asked about the fellowship and about Pastor Sam Philip. A long time ago they shared the same room in Delhi. That's not what is interesting. I sensed a discontent in his voice throughout. He was speaking as though Pastor Philip had done some injustice to Pastor Ko. I did not understand anything beyond that.'

'Is this Jacob Chettan someone who came into the fold of faith?' Rithu asked.

'Not only that, I think he is active in all the organizations and activities of the church.'

'Really? That is really intriguing, Jane. The driver of a pastor who was internationally renowned was the room-mate of a pastor who is well known across India. How did such a person not become a believer? That could be an interesting thing to find out,' said Rithu.

'It is interesting, all right. But don't keep changing the course of your investigation based on everything you hear – you will not get anywhere,' said Jane.

Rithu too felt that Jane was right. You always need someone with you who will think differently from the way you do. Only then will you realize when your thinking is going awry.

'Jacob Chettan had been a driver in Delhi for a long time. He too spoke to me about Midhun. As the pastor says, if you place your trust in the police and sit quiet, nothing will happen. There are two petrol pumps before and after the spot where the accident occurred. His contention is that if the CCTV footage in these pumps is reviewed, we will be able to find the vehicle that knocked Midhun down,' said Jane.

'Usually, once we are in the fold of the fellowship, we don't listen to people from outside. Everything starts and ends with us. We'll change that for once, right?' said Rithu, laughing. Jane laughed too.

'We need to start from the beginning again, Jane. In our journey so far, we've gathered many nuggets of information. We don't know if they can all be connected meaningfully or if certain nuggets are valuable or not. We will know this only when we try to link them all together. I think I am ready to start doing that. But I will need your cooperation, Jane. Now that I have earned your trust, I need you to tell me all that you are still withholding deep inside you. Only then will this journey of ours have meaning.'

Rithu was silent for a couple of minutes, giving Jane the time that she needed to think in peace.

'If a suspicion takes root in your mind, you will try to connect it to everything that follows. That's all there is to this too, Rithu. I am talking about Midhun's medical examination. Sugar, cholesterol, BP, ESR and so on – it was just a routine check-up. The kinds of tests you would do at that age if you are a regular reader of health magazines that create anxiety about your health in you. However, when I connect the accident that happened two days after these tests, the brain death and the organ donation, there is a nagging suspicion in my mind that refuses to go away. Did it all unfold like a pre-planned play? Did Midhun become an unsuspecting actor in a play written by someone else? It might not be anything, Rithu. I told you – suspicion. That's all it is. But my loyalty lies with the hospital. To my source of livelihood. Which is why I did not share all this with anyone so far.'

'For the time being, let that suspicion remain between just the two of us. We'll make an earnest attempt to find that vehicle.'

46

'There is an Italian movie titled *Il Postino*. The movie tells the story of the friendship between the Chilean poet Pablo Neruda and Mario Rupolo, a postman. It was after postponing an emergency heart operation which doctors insisted on that Massimo Troisi, the famous actor, arrived to play the role of the postman. Troisi passed away just twelve hours after the shoot ended. In front of this man who bravely risked his very existence to breathe life into a character, how can we continue to hide in safe zones, how can we be proud of ourselves, Jane?' Rithu asked, as they waited for the signal to change in their journey to find the exact site of the accident.

Nobody had a clear idea of the spot where the accident had occurred – not even Sandhya and Ragesh. Rithu had checked with both of them – and both of them confessed that they did not know the exact location. All they knew was that it was somewhere near the CNG filling station next to the Club Road flyover. Rithu decided that she would take Jane along and take a look anyway. Jane asked her a question: 'Since the day I met you, I've been noticing that you always have a story or an incident that you can give as an example. From where did you get all this knowledge?'

'Cinema. Literature. Music. I have had a fascination for all of it since childhood. And Kurian Sir was a father who encouraged everything happily. I grew up in a room filled with books and films. It was after I came into the fellowship that everything ended. We have been indoctrinated to believe that reading anything other than the Bible is a crime. Since then, I very often feel that life has somehow become too narrow. To be with Christ is what is best for a believer; the rest has to be dismissed as the Devil's work.'

They discovered the landmark they were looking for – the CNG filling station. Driving in, they tried to meet the manager on the pretext of enquiring about the price of distilled water for the car battery. They spoke to the boy who was in charge of refuelling. They tried to find out if he knew where the accident had happened. He did not remember any such event. In the meantime, Rithu discovered that the station had a CCTV camera facing the road. That was all they needed. They left knowing that they might have to come regularly to the gas station for the next few days. A short distance ahead, they saw another petrol pump. They dropped in there too, in an attempt to establish a first contact. But even there, the attendant didn't have any idea about the accident.

'There are a lot of accidents that happen on this road every day. Who can remember them all?' said Jane, defending the attendants.

'If what the driver Jacob Chettan from Bhopal said is correct, the accident happened between these two pumps which are one and a half kilometres apart. That should be easy to find … We need to see the CCTV footage in both the pumps and find the vehicle that was responsible for the accident,' said Rithu. 'I am going to attempt an experiment. Jane, just monitor this,' she said, handing her mobile phone over to Jane after tapping on the stopwatch. She then increased the throttle until the speed touched hundred kmph and stopped in front of the gas station. 'Fifty-four seconds,' said Jane. They drove back at sixty kmph. 'Ninety seconds. But I don't get what you're trying to get out of this.' Jane feared that Rithu was losing her way again. Rithu ignored her. 'Almost all vehicles on this highway travel between sixty and hundred kilometres per hour. What that means is that every car recorded by the camera in the pump should have been recorded by the camera in the gas station somewhere between fifty-four and ninety seconds later. So, if we check the footage starting thirty minutes before the accident, we can get an idea of the vehicle involved in the accident.'

'Really Rithu? Are you serious? Have you decided to inspect these videos and identify the vehicle involved? I am scared. If they know that I am involved in all this, I will surely be in danger.' Jane was on the verge of tears.

'I will find that vehicle, Jane. I just wanted you to understand that, even if just the two of us put our minds to it, we can find this out without anyone else's help. So if the police says that they can't track this, it just means that a lot of money has changed hands. To figure out who gave the money and why, I need to track down the vehicle. I believe the real reason behind Midhun's death is hidden there.'

PART NINE | *Pune*

47

Days later, Rithu received a message from Ragesh. 'I was trying hard not to reach out to you. I even thought that my routine would go on as before though you were not there. But I can't. An emptiness haunts me. I can't concentrate on work in office. I can't be at peace in moments of solitude. I can't focus during the prayer sessions. I get a feeling that I have failed. Kiran's suicide was always the issue that haunted me more than Midhun's death. I keep asking myself why he did that. When I saw his room that day, with Reshma written all over the walls as though he just couldn't find more space to pour his love out, when I saw her images pasted on the roof of his room, I thought almost contemptuously that this was all sheer madness. But now I understand. I understand what he must have felt when he lost Reshma. A lost love can be a bittersweet memory for a woman. But it is not so for a man. It's like the fear of failure for him. Can't you save me from the fear of this downward spiral, Rithu? At least to be kind. Remember, once I wept and said that I just needed an iota of your love – will you deny me that too?'

Rithu got really alarmed that morning when she read Ragesh's message which had landed on her phone sometime during the night. It was not the memories of love or the pain of loss that alarmed her. It was the overwhelming presence of Kiran and his room. Death was alive there. It was to overcome this that Ragesh had joined the fellowship. But did his words not reveal that the fear, like stone, still weighed him down? Rithu was scared of men. She had come to a simple conclusion: that men were pompous asses who had no idea how to face life. Because they could not look life in the eye with as much courage as women could. Ragesh was one of them. She called him right away. Ragesh picked up the call on the first ring, almost as though he was waiting with one finger on the answer key the whole night, and mumbled a sheepish hello. Rithu felt somewhat relieved. That he was still alive. She did not enquire after him or console him; she yelled the choicest of abuses at him, at every man who starts out happily to drink the sweet nectar of love and then begins to sob when he realizes that it is also bitter. Ragesh, quite unlike his usual manly self, sat listening quietly to all the yelling. The thought that she had fallen in love with a nincompoop who would not react to being yelled at, enraged Rithu even more. When she finally rid herself of all her anger, she just said, 'Okay. Since you spent the whole night whimpering, why don't you go get some sleep? We'll meet in the evening,' and hung up.

When they met in the evening, it was as though they had forgotten all about the morning. They wondered why they had wasted so many days and filled each other in on everything. Rithu was surprised by one thing – her lack of trust in Ragesh had suddenly vanished. For the same reason, she had no qualms about sharing everything with him – even things that Jesus had sternly bidden not to tell anyone about. She did not count him as 'anyone' among strangers that evening, she counted him as among her own loved ones. She was amazed at how fragile the boundaries were between decisions and actions after she had told him everything. She had been so sure until yesterday that she was never going to share any of this with Ragesh, and that he had gone away forever from her life. One call was all it took to change everything. How fickle life was.

'Someone sent me a video on WhatsApp the other day, Rithu. I think it was someone who did not like the fact that I was part of the fellowship. Since there are many videos going around that decry pastors, their prayers and their healing sessions, I had decided that I would not look at it. In spite of that, I watched it. It was not a pastor, but a girl who was the heroine in this. To be honest, Rithu, I was really embarrassed watching the video. It shows this girl at two different venues where prayer and healing were happening. At the first venue, she says that she had a lump and ulcers in her stomach for two years which were cured by the prayer of the pastor. At the second venue, she says that she had severe headaches and migraines for three years which were cured by the prayers of the pastor. The pastors are the same. The patients are the same. Can you fault people for laughing at this? Why do they insult ordinary believers like us, Rithu? Why don't they realize the effort we put in to clear the ground we stand on? Pastors who shoot down people – bang, bang – like animated characters in films and drive the Devil away. Pastors who make poor people jump around to exorcize spirits. Pastors who put everyone to sleep with the wave of a hand. Pastors who yell and scream in the name of God. In this age of information and social media, do these pastors think that they can get away with this kind of fraud? I suddenly realized that it was right of you to move away from all this. And from that moment, I've been wanting to see you.'

Thinking that Rithu did not quite believe him, Ragesh showed her the video. To begin with, she was not really amused. But with each passing moment, her eyes widened. It was not because of the racket that was unfolding before her eyes; it was because she knew the girl who was acting as the patient very well. She was Rithu's friend in Pune – Pretty.

48

'My God! You found that on the internet? What else do you need to die of shame? I don't know what's wrong with these people.' Pretty seemed worried at first and then she burst out laughing. She was speaking to Rithu, who had called her in a state of shock after seeing the video.

Ragesh had just left, saying on his way out, 'We need to find the truth behind this, Rithu. We came into the fold. Each of us had our own reasons for doing so. But why should we allow ourselves to become a laughing stock in society?'

Rithu called Pretty as soon as she stepped into her room, even before changing. She was really anxious. But Pretty condensed her reply into a laugh.

'Don't laugh, Pretty, I have still not recovered from the shock,' said Rithu, scolding her.

'It's because you are used to seeing only small things that shock you. It's like how you shiver when you step into the water for the first time. But after you've been in it for a while, you begin to realize that this feeling is not really as big a deal as you thought it to be, that it is just a house of cards built on a foundation of lies,' said Pretty.

'That was from a play I was part of in my early days in Pune. I had no option but to don a role. I have spoken to you in detail about the circle of fate that I am trapped in. They made me play this role. The pastor's take was that all this was required to bring people into the fellowship. In the beginning, I was hesitant. After several shows, it became a joke. A joke that fetched me decent pocket money. Then why give it up? It was not just me, Rithu. There were a few of us. We performed across north India, all the while exchanging roles and illnesses. They needed helpless souls to enact madness, utter gibberish, dance like people possessed and faint when required. Most of them were actors hired from the villages of north India and Tamil Nadu. I don't know if you will believe me when I tell you this – we even had secret camps that taught these actors to faint and dance as though they were possessed. Those were the days when I actually lived out the irony in the Shakespearean lines which I had studied in the eighth standard – "All the world's a stage and all the men and women merely players." It is because you are relatively new seekers that you don't know all this. In fact, it continues to happen even now. If you come to Pune once again, we can go together to see the training ground for God's miracles. If you want, I can give you the opportunity to talk about the miracles of God at one or two venues. There's a very strong market for beautiful women like you.'

For a long time, Rithu sat in silence with the phone in her hand. Long enough to make Pretty wonder if she had hung up and gone. 'Amidst all this, where does the Christ who was crucified belong, Pretty?' Rithu eventually asked.

Pretty burst out laughing again. 'This is the age of tele-evangelists who travel the world in their private jets, charging crores for a one-hour session on TV. What business does that poor carpenter from Nazareth have here? The poor man is probably standing inconspicuously amidst people, worried if he will be done to death again.' Pretty laughed again, and that was the end of that conversation.

'How can she laugh in spite of all this?' Ragesh asked, when Rithu called him to fill him in on her conversation with Pretty.

'It is possible, Ragesh. Miracles will stun us and secrets will shock us only up to a point. After that, you just feel like laughing at it all. Pretty has pretty much crossed that point after traversing through surprise and shock. We should not make light of her laughter. It contains the weight of all the miseries that she has carried,' said Rithu.

'I don't know the nature of the investigation you are undertaking into Midhun's death or where it has reached. But from tomorrow onwards, I will be with you on this,' Ragesh assured Rithu firmly, before he wound up the conversation that night.

'You still live in my heart with the same passion, as you did yesterday. In every way.' It was after sending this message to Ragesh that Rithu went to bed.

49

Three days later, when Rithu met Ragesh in the evening at a restaurant, he had a mug of beer in front of him. Though he was a fan of BBC, he had avoided beer and cricket since he had come into the fellowship. The only time Rithu remembered seeing him drink was in her own house in Goa, when Kurian Sir served local feni and beef roast. She'd ignored it in the overall revelry. 'Normally, men go back to drinking when they are lovelorn. What's wrong with you now? Are you sad that I'm back in your life?' she teased.

'No! This is the result of a book I just read. The revolutionary pastor Martin Luther had three lines on his beer mug. He used to joke that the first line represented the ten commandments, the second line the law of faith of the Apostles and the third the prayer of Christ. While certain friends could not even cross "the ten commandments", he could easily reach "the prayer of Christ". If the true representative of God can, why can't I, a mere seeker? I thought I'd find out how far I'd be able to travel during this happy hour, when you get two for the price of one. That's all,' said Ragesh, gulping down a mouthful of beer.

'It is not for nothing that the pastor banned us from reading other books! He probably knew that people like you would only see the darker side of things. And one more thing – Martin Luther, the leader of the Protestant revolution has no connection with our fellowship. Our roots go back to Charles Palm, of the Methodist Ministry in America. Don't be shocked that I know this – I got this information a while ago from one of Kurian Sir's books.'

'Why did you not stumble upon the story of that beer mug in any of those books? How many days I wasted. Beef and beer are now okay. I just need to find out about cricket,' Ragesh sighed. 'Anyway, forget all that. If you find out what your future husband did over the last two days, you'd give me a hug and a kiss right away.'

'What is the great thing that my boyfriend did that makes him dream of something that is really unlikely to happen?'

'I went to both the pumps, bribed the staff and copied the CCTV footage during the time of Midhun's accident. I sat and watched the entire footage without even going to work yesterday. And I've made a note of something that looks suspicious. Is all this not enough to warrant a kiss from my girlfriend?' Ragesh pushed back his collar in a show of pride.

'Now I know that you have a place in the list of useless boyfriends – the kind who will get on his bike at midnight and go in search of a rose if his girlfriend demands to inhale its fragrance. Stop flirting and tell me what you found out,' said Rithu.

'From what I saw, two vehicles look suspicious to me. I'll show it to you as well and then come to a conclusion,' Ragesh said, as though he was a hotshot investigating officer. 'I don't think there is much use in showing it to me – nevertheless, let's take a look,' said Rithu. Ragesh showed her the video that was saved on his tablet. In the first video, she could clearly see Midhun on a bike, followed by a jeep and, a bit later, by a lorry. In the video from the second pump, the bike was not there. The lorry went by first, followed by the jeep. The footage from both the cameras revealed that no other vehicle had passed by for a while after this.

'Would it have been the lorry or the jeep that hit Midhun's bike? What's your take?' Ragesh asked, switching off the tab.

'Since you've watched this footage many times, tell me your take first,' Rithu said.

'I think it was the lorry driver. After that, he increased speed and overtook the jeep. If it was the jeep, the lorry driver would have seen and reported it – which has not happened. It was the lorry driver,' Ragesh said.

'I want to see the video once again,' said Rithu, and taking the tablet from Ragesh, watched the footage again.

'Prima facie, your inference seems to be correct. But I see it in a different way. Look, the first camera shows Midhun's bike passing by in the afternoon at 3:17:22. The jeep passes by at 3:17:28. And the lorry at 3:17:43. Now look at the footage from the second camera. Midhun's bike does not appear here. The lorry passes by at 3:18:32 – he took just forty-nine seconds. The jeep passes by at 3:19:33 – he took a hundred and twenty-five seconds. The other day, Jane and I checked this out – if you are travelling at hundred kmph, it takes fifty-four seconds to cover the distance between the two cameras. At sixty kmph, it takes ninety seconds. So if the lorry covered this distance in forty-nine seconds, that means he was travelling at slightly over one hundred kmph. Which means the lorry overtook Midhun as well as the jeep. If the lorry had hit Midhun's bike, the driver of the jeep would definitely have seen that – this has not happened. Now look at the jeep – even if it were moving at sixty kmph, it would have been captured by the second camera after ninety seconds. But the jeep took a hundred and twenty-five seconds. Which means the jeep slowed down in between. This could be because he gave way to the lorry. And then hit Midhun's bike and sped on. There is one other thing that proves that in this video. In the footage from the first camera, the speed of the jeep is not high – but in the second, it is very high. You can almost see the impatience to get away from the scene.'

'Brilliant! That's outstanding deduction. So we can focus on just the jeep, right?' Ragesh asked.

'I wouldn't say that. But the jeep definitely looks more suspicious.'

50

'Every question has two answers. The right one and the polite one. The person who asks the question must decide which answer is required.'

This was Midhun's response to Sandhya's question, 'What is it that you desire the most?'

'No. It is not the person who asks the question who decides that. It is the emotional bond between the two people that decides what the answer should be,' Sandhya replied. 'A relationship without depth elicits polite responses.'

Midhun's silence was his affirmation. 'Quenching the desires of my body.' Midhun made this frank statement when Sandhya was expecting reading, writing or biking as an answer. Maybe he saw this as an opportunity to express the depth of their relationship. There was a reason why this conversation was happening. There was an Aunty from Bangalore who used to come once in a while to attend the prayer meetings that were held in Sandhya's house. Even after everyone had left, she would stay on in Sandhya's flat for a while. She would just sit and chat, or play with Sandhya's daughter. Sandhya and this Aunty became quite close. Close enough to share

personal experiences. Which is why she disclosed her reason
for joining the fellowship as well as for staying on at Sandhya's
flat long after the prayer meeting was over.'I too had that kind
of a desire, Sandhya, around the time I was newly married.
A desire that would not go away even if I fulfilled it once or
twice. But after I had two children, there was a coldness that
enveloped my body. I lost interest in it. But the desire of my
husband, who was the sales manager in a premium textile
shop, just kept rising. After talking, listening and interacting
with women of all ages who would come searching for different
trends in fashion all through the day, he would come home in
the evening, filled with desire. And then, before his bath, after
his bath, before dinner, after dinner, before falling asleep, after
waking up – it was when I realized that my body would not
be able to take it any more, that I started faking a certain kind
of madness. Grinding my teeth, making faces, rolling my eyes,
sticking my tongue out, drooling, screaming without reason
and so on. The only way to save my body was to pretend that
I was possessed. That is when some friend told him about the
pastor and I was brought to his healing camp. That day too, I
put on a sterling performance. It was as though all the devils in
the world had possessed me. The pastor prayed and healed me
that day. I laugh when I think of all that – I know that he has
not rid my body of even one devil. What he drove away was
the Devil in my husband's body. He became a great admirer
of the pastor. And I was relieved. That's how I became a
permanent member of the fellowship. It was not to attain any
heaven – it was just to sleep peacefully at home every night.

But the beast in man has no option but to wake up. That is his basic behaviour. I can no longer act like I am possessed. But it is to stay away from home as much as possible that I come for meetings. And then stay on here without going back, playing with this child. You understand my situation, don't you?'

Sandhya could not help but share this story with Midhun. Those were the days when Midhun had found his way to Sandhya's bed to explore desires, triggered by a line in a Kazantzakis novel that both of them were reading at the same time. It was Sandhya's comment that Midhun was also becoming like that Aunty's husband that started the conversation which ended with him saying nothing more than 'Quenching the desires of my body.'

Sandhya was reminded of all this many, many days later when Ragesh and Rithu dropped in at her apartment one evening. She had heard that they had fallen apart for sometime in between. She'd wanted to call and find out what had happened – but somehow she never got around to it. Probably because the numbness in her mind had slowly enveloped her whole being. That day, when she saw them together, she was happy. They sat and talked like they used to long ago, without anyone mentioning the falling-out in between. They had coffee on the balcony. Shared the information they had about Midhun's death. 'You've been in this space for a while. Have you not come upon any new information?' Sandhya asked.

'We have taken one small step forward. We zoomed in on the vehicle and, though a bit hazy, we managed to figure out the registration number of the jeep.'

'So we can be sure of the vehicle, right?' Sandhya asked with sudden interest.

'Yes. But what is interesting is not that, Sandhya. Remember the Aunty from Bangalore who used to come to our prayer meetings? Jovana Xavier. The jeep belongs to her husband. Her home address in the fellowship's register and the address to which that jeep is registered are the same. You know her well, don't you? You should call her and find out if they still have the jeep and who drives it.'

'Now?' Sandhya asked a bit doubtfully.

'Yes. Who knows about tomorrow?' Ragesh insisted.

Sandhya fished out the number from the fellowship's directory and called Aunty Jovana. She started complaining about the broken prayer group and said that she was part of another group now. Sandhya reassured her saying that the old prayer group would be revived and insisted that she come back to this group. 'Can I rent out your jeep? It's to go to Kasol with a few friends.'

'Oh Sandhya, that was sold about six months ago,' she said apologetically.

'Ask who it was sold to,' Ragesh prompted Sandhya.

'It was some north Indian. Let Xavier come back, I'll check with him and let you know.' Aunty hung up.

'So the vehicle has been sold. But the ownership has not changed. We have three new questions now. Who bought the jeep? Why has the ownership remained unchanged? Is that intentional or just sheer laziness?'

Sandhya continued to sit in her balcony long after Ragesh and Rithu had left, without even getting up to close the door. Her mind was suddenly full of Midhun. She thought of the nights they had spent discovering each other. She sat there and dreamt of his desires enveloping her. She felt as if the fireflies playing around the branches of the tall tree outside had emanated from her body.

PART TEN

Delhi

51

There was an article tucked away inside the next day's newspaper. It was sheer chance that Ragesh, who never had the habit of reading the newspaper, saw it at all. The story was all about how a kidney racket had been busted at a very prestigious hospital in Delhi. A brawl between the donor and the middlemen regarding the payment brought the police into the picture and then, when they were questioned, a sordid, shocking story came out. The news story ended by saying that five doctors, including senior nephrologist Dr Ashok Charan, were booked and a case registered at the Sarita Vihar police station.

As the newspapers seemed to know, for a seasoned Delhiite, this was not a shocking news story. It was common knowledge that many such mutually beneficial projects thrived in every hospital. What struck Ragesh was that, among those arrested, there was a Xavier. Ragesh was suddenly suspicious. Was this Aunty Jovana's husband? He called Rithu and shared the news. 'There are thousands of Xaviers in Delhi. This might be an unfounded suspicion,' said Rithu, dismissively. In spite of that, they got Sandhya to call Aunty Jovana about the jeep.

Her voice instantly revealed that the Xavier arrested was indeed her husband. All upset, she sobbed into the phone, 'Xavier is not someone like that – somebody cheated him.'

'We should go and console her – after all, she was part of our prayer group', suggested Ragesh. Sandhya and Rithu agreed.

Two days later, when they went to Aunty Jovana's flat, Xavier was also there. They hadn't expected that he would be able to get himself out so quickly. A visibly upset Xavier said that a few influential people had managed to bail him out and that he would now have to pursue the case for years on end. They were relieved to see Sandhya, Ragesh and Rithu. 'Of late, he really was not interested in prayer or the fellowship – this is Jesus's way of punishing him. Praise the Lord,' said Aunty Jovana. Xavier explained that he had gone for a regular check-up to the hospital. It was when the altercation broke out and he went over to find out what was happening, that the police arrested him. Ragesh slowly turned the conversation towards the jeep. Both Rithu and Ragesh felt that he was trying to avoid that topic by saying that it was some north Indian who had bought it.

'You should be careful, Uncle. The ownership has not been transferred yet. If the new owner is involved in an accident, that too will become your headache,' said Ragesh, and it had its effect. The three of them saw fear flit by on Xavier's face.

'That sale was arranged by Brother Aruldas of our fellowship. I must talk to him and trace the owner,' Xavier said, almost to himself. Then he asked, anxiously, 'Why, do you have information that my jeep was in some accident?' None of the three friends said anything. They tried to scare Xavier a bit more by glancing at each other furtively and contributing to an uneasy silence. They realized that their strategy had worked when they saw the look on Xavier's face.

For the first time since they started the investigation, they had a feeling that they were getting somewhere. They parted happily that evening. Later that night, Pretty called Rithu from Pune, to say that Xavier, who belonged to their fellowship, was entangled in a kidney racket. 'No, Uncle is a good guy. He got entangled in it for no fault of his,' Rithu defended Xavier intentionally.

'If you guys believed him, he should get the Oscar for best actor, no doubt. Rithu, he is definitely a part of that racket. The job in the textile shop is just a cover. If you are wondering how I know all this sitting in Pune, I would suggest you go meet Jane as soon as you can. She will tell you more.'

Rithu couldn't sleep any more. The fact that she could not get Jane on the phone made things worse.

Next morning, Rithu went to the hospital on her scooty. Though it was not visiting hours, she managed to get in using Dr John Samuel's name and managed to track Jane down in front of the operation theatre.

'Rithu, I know why you kept calling me. And that is exactly why I did not answer. Please don't put me in a fix. The fact that we are standing here and having a conversation is being recorded by CCTV cameras. I am scared.'

Jane was on the verge of tears. But Rithu was not ready to give up. 'I will be waiting outside when your duty is over. Don't try to vanish. Wherever you go, I'll find you.' Rithu's voice had the authority of a police officer.

'No. Don't come here. I will come to our usual Subway,' Jane relented.

'Fine. I'll be there,' said Rithu and left the hospital.

In the evening, Rithu picked Jane up from the Subway and went straight to Sandhya's flat, where Ragesh was also waiting.

'I made the mistake of telling Pretty yesterday that Xavier is not as innocent as we believe him to be. You cannot crucify me like this for that,' Jane cried.

'Jane, don't think that we are torturing you emotionally. It is not when we shout out prayers four times a day, but when we work and share things for the good of everyone that we become more dear to God.'

Jane went silent for a minute when she heard Ragesh's words. And then she said, 'What Pretty said is true. He is not so innocent ... I have personal experience. Many a time, the hospital will need a kidney for transplant. Xavier is the main guy who brings in donors. And he will extract his commission from all three people – the donor, the recipient and the hospital. A man like that can definitely be suspected of being part of a racket.'

'Then how did he get bail so quickly?' Sandhya asked.

'Ah! Do you not live in this world? If the beggar mafia can protect a man who killed a girl, you can easily guess the kind of influence these people will have.'

'He was complaining that nobody from the fellowship enquired after him,' Rithu said.

'That complaint shows that he is an outstanding crook,' Jane said, sipping the coffee that Sandhya had served. On the day this happened, I was on duty in Dr Samuel's Out-Patient. The whole day he was on the phone like a madman. I think he would have even called the prime minister's office to get him out.'

'What is the doctor's interest in this?'

'That is something you can guess. Do I have to spell it out?'

'Why can't you just say it? Who is it that you fear?'

'I have signed a contract which says that I will not reveal anything that happens in the hospital to anyone. My fear stems from the fact that I really do not know what the punishment will be if I flout the contract. There is no point in knowing the secrets of powerful people. Even if we try to know them, it will be in vain – they will continue to remain secrets forever. So I don't understand why we are chasing all this. The best way to ensure peace today and henceforth is to come to terms with the fact that we have lost the people we have lost and just let go,' said Jane.

'I don't want that kind of peace, Jane. I have to find out the real people behind this loss.' The fact that this was said by Sandhya, who had been taking things really slow until then, came as a big surprise to the rest of them.

52

The following morning, Rithu received an unexpected call from Kurian Sir. Usually, it was only when Rithu called him that they talked and exchanged all the news. The useless habit of calling children every other minute to track them had been nipped successfully in the bud by Rithu. Which is why his call, even before she had really opened her eyes in the morning, surprised her.

'Nothing. Once you reach the office, you won't be reachable – so I thought I'd call you now. That project I had undertaken – the one about Pastor Alvares – it went to print yesterday. So I thought I'd inform the translator who worked on it,' Kurian Sir said. Rithu's irritation at having been woken up vanished in an instant.

'Congratulations, Kurian Sir, on having completed – for the first time – a project that you took up! As soon as it comes out, you should courier two copies of the book to me. I need to read it out to a few people here. They will then get an idea of what charity is, what selfless service is and what spirituality is.'

Before Kurian Sir could say, 'When will you be coming home next?' Rithu hung up and answered a call that had been waiting for a while. It was Ragesh. Her boyfriend decided to act slightly wounded because her phone had been engaged so early in the morning. 'Who were you speaking to at this odd hour? Is your heart hooked on to someone whose voice you have to hear first thing in the morning?'

'Get lost, you suspicious idiot. That is a man to whom my heart has always been hooked – my Papa. He called to tell me that a book of his will soon be released.' Rithu, who never gave explanations about anything she did in her life, was very accommodating of Ragesh that morning. But he was calling for a different reason. 'It was our Brother Aruldas who bailed Xavier out. Xavier's lies are falling apart. If you can take leave today, we can go meet Aruldas.'

'Won't happen, Ragesh. The guys in the office will shoot me if I so much as say the word "leave". And yes, I can tell you what Aruldas's response will be right now. "If someone in the fellowship is in danger, is it not our duty to help and support him? That is not because of any questionable association." Don't expect anything else from any of them, Ragesh. It is only people who feel bad about telling a lie who will at least feel a pang of guilt. The majority of people in our fellowship firmly believe that whatever they are doing is right.'

'Maybe, Rithu. But thus far, I have not really felt that Brother Aruldas is such a person. And that is what gives me confidence. I believe we will get to hear the secrets that we have all been waiting for from him.'

'The reply you need has already been given by Jesus Christ: your faith will save you.'

Even though Rithu said that and hung up, she realized that there was indeed some logic in what Ragesh had said. Meeting Brother Aruldas could shed more light on what they were seeking. She went to the office in that hope. She had to switch off her mobile inside the office, had to disconnect from the world when she stepped in to work. She would switch it on later, only on her way to the canteen for lunch. A message that had been sent earlier landed on her phone.

'Ragesh's life is in danger. Be very careful.'

The message had come from the same number from which she was earlier asked if they had found the vehicle which had hit Midhun. Rithu was terrified. She called Ragesh immediately. His phone was switched off. That doubled her fear. She tried to call Sandhya, but she was out of reach. Rithu's heart was racing. She tried sending a message to Ragesh on WhatsApp. That was delivered. But he was not looking at it. She called him on WhatsApp. Then on Messenger. Then on Hangouts. But he did not come online or take her calls. She was at her wits' end. If a friend goes offline, then how can you trace him? That suddenly seemed to be the most frustrating question she had ever faced. She sat and sweated in the air-conditioned canteen. She felt faint. And weak. She went to the loo three or four times. To a few colleagues who knew of their friendship, Rithu just said that Ragesh was not reachable. She could not reveal anything more. 'He might be in a place where there is no signal. Try calling after a while,' they said lightly. She tried to take a half-day leave a couple of times. But that did not work. She somehow managed to push through the workday. And like children who snatch their bags and run as soon as the national anthem is over, she ran out of office as soon as it was punch-out time. No sooner had she reached the parking lot, than she tried calling Ragesh. His phone rang. And in a while she heard him say hello. Rithu felt unbelievably relieved, almost as though someone had poured an entire bucket of water on her.

'Where were you all this while?' She was really yelling.

'There was an accident. I couldn't inform you,' Ragesh said.

'Ragesh, please, are you hurt?' Rithu cried.

'Not me. Our Brother Aruldas is gone.'

'Gone? What are you saying?' Rithu was so anxious she could hardly speak.

'Yes. He fell out of the train on his way to Chennai this morning. This happened in Agra. I am here now. The post-mortem just got over. If possible, the body will be sent home today.'

'What are you doing there? You are not doing the post-mortem, are you? Come back as soon as you can. I want to see you now!' Rithu was crying like a stubborn child.

'Rithu, I am standing in the veranda of a government hospital. Someone we know very well is lying in the mortuary. How can I come there now? Don't be like a little child. Don't we have a responsibility towards our people?'

'I don't want to hear your logic. If you love me, please come back to Delhi immediately. One more thing – don't tell anyone that you are coming back. And use some mode of public transport.'

'What do you mean? What is the matter, Rithu?'

'Ragesh, for now, just know that danger is stalking us.' Rithu was almost whispering.

'I am more aware of that than you. I will do as you say. I'm coming. I have quite a lot to share.'

'What?' Rithu asked anxiously.

'I spoke to Brother Aruldas in the morning. I'll tell you everything once I get back.'

'I'm going to Sandhya's flat. You come there. I will rest only after I see you.'

53

By the time Ragesh returned, it was past midnight. Until then, Sandhya was busy trying to pacify Rithu. In spite of seeing Ragesh unharmed, it took another five minutes for Rithu to really calm down. It was only then that she revealed the real reason why she was so anxious and scared. She showed Ragesh and Sandhya the message she had received in the morning.

'This is someone playing a prank on us,' Sandhya said, trying to make light of the situation.

'That is what even I thought until now. But it's not like that Sandhya,' Ragesh said gravely. 'I met Brother Aruldas this morning. He told me that there was truth behind these messages.'

'Does that mean that it was Brother Aruldas himself?' Rithu stood up in anxiety.

'He did not say that. And he did not deny it either. But he was clearly aware of these messages.'

'What did he say about the jeep? Any idea who bought it?' Rithu asked.

'It was Advocate Ram Manohar Varma who told Brother Aruldas that he needs such a vehicle urgently for an acquaintance. This was one week before Midhun's accident. The vehicle was picked up by a workshop owner from Old Delhi. Contacting him will give us an idea of where exactly this vehicle is now. But Brother Aruldas discouraged me from pursuing that lead. When I really put pressure on him though, he gave me the address of the person, after making me promise that I would tell no one in this world that I had got the address from him. He said that he was going to Chennai urgently today and that, upon his return, he would speak to me about a few other things. And later, I heard that he had fallen off the train.'

'When did you meet him?' asked Rithu, as if something suddenly occurred to her.

'Within about half an hour of our conversation in the morning. I had no peace without knowing the story of the jeep. I went right away and met him.'

Rithu examined the message that she had received once again. 'Look at the time at which this message was sent. According to what you said, Ragesh, this message was sent immediately after the two of you met. So there is no need to go anywhere in search of the person who sent it.'

That is when Sandhya picked up her phone as though she had suddenly remembered something and started looking at her own messages. 'Remember, without any reason, all of us drifted apart. I had received a message during those days. At that time, I did not take it seriously. But the way things are now, that message might open another door for us. I don't think I deleted it,' said Sandhya, without taking her eyes off her phone.

'Let me complete', Ragesh interrupted. 'I went in search of the workshop guy immediately. He told me that the jeep was involved in a bad accident last week and, since it was unrepairable, he sold it as scrap. He showed me a certificate from the vehicle inspector stating that the registration had been cancelled. The workshop owner claims that he did not bother to change the ownership certificate because of this.'

'Which means all the evidence we have is vanishing into thin air, right?' Sandhya asked, while still searching for the message on her mobile.

'Yes. With today's accident, the evidence called Aruldas has also been done away with.'

'But who's behind all this?'

'Rithu, those names are on the tip of your tongue as well as on mine. But because we don't have real proof, we are hesitant to take their names even between us.'

'But I can't understand why they would want to do all this, Ragesh.'

'There too, a few pointers and probabilities have emerged clearly. All we need to do is confirm them.'

'Got it!' Sandhya got up, excited at having having found the message she was looking for. 'Jacob. Dayal Pharmaceuticals. This man might be able to help you a great deal' – was the message that had been sleeping in Sandhya's phone for a long time.

'Jacob! This is a name we have come across in the last few days,' Ragesh said, thinking furiously. But none of them succeeded in recollecting anything specific.

'It's late. Do you want to go home now?' Sandhya asked, serving Ragesh chapatis and vegetable curry, even though he said he was not hungry.

'We'll go. Have to go to office in the morning,' said Ragesh. But Rithu disagreed.

'We're not going anywhere tonight. Just give us a bed sheet each.'

That night, the three of them spread sheets on the floor and slept in the small living room of Sandhya's flat. All of them ended up thinking and talking about the fourth person who should have been with them.

54

It was while she was hurrying to the office on her scooty, wondering if she would be late to punch in, that Rithu suddenly remembered who the person called Jacob was. And then, for a while, she thought of the moment that triggered this memory. Last night, while the three of them were talking, one part of Rithu's mind was deep-diving into the past to figure out who Jacob was. Yet, it was when she was speeding to work thinking only of punching in on time that the memory surfaced. She was baffled by the pathways the mind used to travel inwards and find what one was looking for. It happened when she saw the Subway delivery box on a two-wheeler by the roadside. She then thought of Jane, and then thought of Jane's trip to Bhopal for Aunty Annie's funeral. Then she remembered that Jane had met a person called Jacob there. Could the Jacob in Sandhya's message be the same Jacob? Would he have met and spoken to Jane intentionally? Rithu parked her scooty on the roadside and called Ragesh.

'I too figured out who Jacob was while I was in the shower. It was based on his recommendation that we went to the two pumps to take a look at the CCTV footage. And that really helped. This could mean that he knows much more,' said Ragesh.

'Then let's call Jacob Chettan, Ragesh.'

'No point, Rithu. Nobody will be willing to disclose any secrets on the mobile any more. We will have to go to Bhopal and speak to him directly.'

'Okay. When can we go? Let me see if I can take leave for one day – even if I have to murder someone in the office for it,' Rithu said.

'No. I'll go and enquire by myself.'

'Alone? Do you think that I'll let you go alone again? You have no idea what I went through yesterday. If we are going, we'll go together.'

'Okay. Let me know which day will work for you. I'll try and locate Jacob by then so that we won't have to wander about in search of him once we get there.'

Rithu fell at the project manager's feet and managed to wrangle twenty-four hours off three days later. And as far as Ragesh was concerned, since he had no interest in continuing in that office or in Delhi, in spite of getting a second reminder, he stayed away from work without even sending an email in response. In the middle of all of this, Ragesh managed to call Dayal Pharmaceuticals, find out the number of the office driver Jacob Chettan, call him and fix up a meeting with him without divulging the reason.

In spite of that, they had to wait until lunchtime for Jacob Chettan to turn up in the visiting room of Dayal Pharmaceuticals. 'The manager had to be taken unexpectedly for a meeting – it was unavoidable. That's why you had to wait.' When Jacob finally turned up, he apologized to them. And then asked why Ragesh and Rithu wanted to meet him with this prelude, 'If it is to sell insurance or teach me what belief is all about, please don't waste time.'

'No, it's not. Don't worry.' Ragesh cut to the chase. 'I'm sure you remember meeting a woman called Jane when you came for Aunty Annie's funeral. We're her friends. To be more precise, we are friends of the late Midhun. We need to find out a few things from you. That's why we came all the way here.'

Jacob Chettan did not respond right away. Instead, he took Ragesh and Rithu in the office car to a restaurant and bought them jeera rice and mutton curry. He then took them to his apartment. It was a run-down flat without too many conveniences, in a narrow street in old Bhopal.

'I am aware of the limitations of my flat. But this is the best place to sit and talk – which is why I brought you here,' said Jacob, giving them an inkling of what to expect as they climbed up the stairs to the second floor, flagged on one side with walls and corners stained with betel-juice.

'If you had set your mind to it, you could have avoided the death of Brother Aruldas,' Jacob Chettan said, without any preamble.

'How?' Ragesh and Rithu were stunned.

'It is when criminals suspect they are being pursued that they start destroying evidence.' They did not respond to that. 'Okay, now tell me what you want to know from me. Ask.'

'Jacob Chettan, why did you give up Delhi and shift to Bhopal? What is your relationship with Pastor Sam Philip? Why didn't you join the fellowship even though you were Pastor Ko Hee-sung's driver for so many years? Who is responsible for Midhun's death?'

Jacob Chettan got up to fetch a Bible. 'This is the Bible that you and I believe in. Only if you swear upon this Bible that you agree to two conditions of mine, will this conversation go forward. If not, we'll go down, have a cup of tea and part ways.'

For a split second, the duo were reluctant. And then, without caring for the consequences, they placed their hands on the Bible.

'One: You should stop your investigation after this. Two: You should leave Delhi and go to some other state.' Both of them nodded their heads like little children before a school teacher.

'I was in Delhi for twelve years. Of those, I was Pastor Ko's driver for eight years. All along, we had a good relationship going – I was not far removed from his belief. So it would be wrong to say that I was not a believer. I guess he believed that I too would come forward on my own to be baptized one day, like Shanu, the Hindi teacher who became a pastor. But that did not happen. It was during that time that your Pastor Sam Philip landed in Delhi without a penny in his pocket or even a change of clothes. He was not Pastor Sam Philip then. He was just Sam – someone who would beg for money from my daily taxi earnings and then run to the bar every evening.

Though he was just a friend's friend, I allowed him to stay with me and gave him food for two years. It was during those days that Pastor Ko made a plan to start a school for poor children and, with the help of the Hong Kong prayer group, decided to buy some land in Shiv Vihar. But a technical problem arose: individuals could not accept large funds from abroad; this could be done only by forming and registering a trust with Indians also on the board. Though Pastor Ko approached many fellowships for the same, it was all in vain because every fellowship wanted permission to utilize the money as they deemed fit. The pastor was cut up about the fact that though a large fund was allocated, it could not be utilized in any way. He had spoken to me many times about it. I would go back home and tell Sam about all this. One day, I heard that Sam had a vision one night and that he went to the pastor's house and got himself baptized. However, I knew that the only vision he had was of the pastor's money. I had mentioned this to the pastor once. But he had already fallen for Sam's ability to talk convincingly. They formed a trust. Money started flowing in from Korea. Slowly, Dr John Samuel and Advocate Ram Manohar Varma became part of the trust. In the end, what I had anticipated happened. Pastor Ko was ousted from the trust. Everything he had worked for and created in the past twenty years, including the fellowship, fell into the hands of this gang. Pastor Ko's attempt to go to court had to be abandoned because, as a foreigner, he could not command the protection of the court. In the end, he left the country, dejected and disappointed. And then the fellowship severed ties with the Hong Kong prayer group and tied up with a prayer group in Philadelphia. There was another thing that happened before all this. I was removed from the post of the driver of Pastor Ko. What was really intriguing was the fact that it was Pastor Philip who took the lead in moving me out because I was not baptized.

'It is not just because it is convenient to sit here and talk that I brought you to my flat. It was also to show you how I am living today. If I had played along with Sam's designs, I could have been living in one of the most plush apartments in Delhi,' Jacob Chettan said, tapping on his chest with his hand. 'Life is not just about money, happiness, prosperity and gains. Life is also about self-respect, honesty and pure faith, without any expectations. I don't regret anything in my life.

'Think about why brain deaths do not occur in government hospitals. You will then understand the reason why Midhun died,' said Jacob Chettan before seeing them off.

PART ELEVEN

Bilaspur

55

A vast majority of women across the world think that a man approaches them only for sex. Because they themselves think that they don't have the right to get anything more. My dear Sandhya, I don't know how you will react to this thought of mine. But this is the response I got from all the women I've had the occasion to talk about love with. I was amazed at how they did not even bother to enquire about what it was that they could give me. But you were different. You understood the desires of my heart. You once asked if I would ever stop loving you. How can one end love, Sandhya? Does the river ever stop flowing? Even if there is nobody to receive her, she will forever keep flowing. But we cannot start any journey knowing how it will end. Go ahead. There will be light on your path. Always. The light of love.

It was when Sandhya was reading an email that Midhun had sent during his last days for the hundredth time, that Ragesh and Rithu walked into her flat. She had no clue about their Bhopal trip until then. 'I called Dayal Pharmaceuticals. There is a Jacob there,' Sandhya said innocently.

Both of them laughed. Sandhya was like a local train that was running really late. They then told her all about their Bhopal trip. Sandhya sat like a frozen frame from the Republic Day parade and listened to them unblinkingly.

'To be honest, we did not come here to tell you this. But to tell you that both of us have decided to leave this city. It's not only because we have to honour the promise we made to Jacob Chettan, but it is also because we have come to hate living in this city. We would like to know your opinion on this.' Sandhya continued to sit quietly for a while.

'You guys have other cities to create nests in. And a home to walk into when you choose to. But my situation? Where can I go if I leave this city? Why, I can't even think of leaving the fellowship. No matter how dangerous a place that is. So long as my daughter is with me, my job is really precious. People who are not alone have limitations in taking decisions. It will be safer for you to forget me.'

'This is not an issue of remembering or forgetting, Sandhya. We are all people who came into this city from different lands. People who are destined to part and continue their journey at some point in time. It is just that this is happening a bit too early,' Rithu said.

'But leaving the task that we undertook halfway is a terrible thing to do, especially to Midhun. Will your conscience allow you to do that?' Sandhya asked.

'Leaving does not mean leaving tomorrow morning. It's just that we took the decision to do so. There are quite a few formalities that have to be completed in the office as well as in the city,' Ragesh said. 'While all this will go on, I am sure that we will complete the task that we undertook. Even if we don't, there is nothing to be disappointed about. Anyone can guess that we are walking towards answers that everyone knows.'

'It's not the answers; it's the reasons, the paths they choose to achieve their ends, the people who are sacrificed for the same – it is towards all these that we need to walk. There was one thing that I was thinking about the whole of last night. This is a gut feeling that comes from my experience. Our Aunty Jovana and Uncle Xavier are not really bad people. If they are, then we will have to say that everyone in this world has two faces. My gut tells me that we need to meet them once more.'

'That might be true, Sandhya. But they are prime suspects right now. All eyes are on them. We need to think of how sensible it will be to go over and meet them at this time.'

'We have a satisfactory explanation for anyone who wants to know. We are all part of the same prayer group. It is the duty of believers to go and comfort people who are going through a bad patch.'

'I think we need to be very cautious because every move of ours is being watched by invisible eyes,' Rithu said. 'Don't think that our opponents are innocent people.'

'Behind every gain there is a loss. Even a thief loses a night of sleep. We won't be able to get anywhere if we decide to play it safe all the way,' replied Sandhya.

'It's funny that you, who are scared of even losing your job, are saying all this.'

'Let's not argue among ourselves. We'll take all decisions unanimously. If that is what you want Sandhya, we will go meet Aunty Jovana once again without thinking of the consequences. And we will find a new job for Sandhya in another city as soon as possible,' said Ragesh, taking this on as his own responsibility.

'It's easy to say that Ragesh. My relationship with Delhi is not one that can be uprooted all that quickly. My daughter studies here. The only roof over my head is in this city. More than all that, the final verdict on my divorce case is still pending. There are many formalities to be completed. I need to produce my daughter in the court. I hope you understand that the problem is not just limited to finding a job?' Sandhya shared her helplessness.

'We'll think about all that later. Right now, we'll make a casual visit to Aunty Jovana's house.' Nobody had a second thought about Rithu's suggestion.

56

They landed at Aunty Jovana's place at a perfect time. She was alone. Xavier had gone out somewhere. They thought that she appeared more tired and sad than when they had met her the last time. She held their hands and wept. From the conversation that ensued, they understood that the death of Brother Aruldas was really haunting her. Rather than say anything about that, they read the Bible for a while, sang hymns and then prayed for Aunty and her family to be saved from sorrow, misery, trials and tribulations. Their life at the fellowship had taught them that the best way to win her over was to do all that. Aunty continued to pray loudly and when she was done, she seemed a bit relieved. She asked how Sandhya's divorce, Rithu's job and Ragesh's diet were going. 'How on earth did Uncle Xavier land in the midst of these crooks, Aunty?' Ragesh slipped in the question at an opportune moment.

'Coming to this city was one wrong thing we did. Xavier had a good job in Bangalore. And a bit of real estate business on the side. It was during that time that we happened to hear one of Pastor Sam Philip's speeches and then started going to the fellowship. Later, once when Pastor Philip came to Bangalore, Dr John Samuel was also with him. After the service, they met Xavier and then came home for dinner the next day. The visit was also to tell us that the doctor wanted to start a hospital in Bangalore and that he would like Xavier to connect him to people who might have the right plot for sale. Xavier facilitated this without much delay. But instead of starting a hospital there, the doctor sold the property later. Xavier was the middleman for that sale as well. And then that became a practice. They cashed in on the land boom, buying and selling many plots. But then, they lost a lot of money on a joint venture. Xavier lost more money than he could imagine. Everything that we had managed to save by working in Bangalore was wiped out. Xavier was neck-deep in debt. There was no way we could stay on in Bangalore. In fact, it was the pastor himself who found a job for Xavier in a textile showroom. After having given up a good job there, everything here was a struggle. I knew that there were still business transactions of some kind going on between Xavier and the doctor. But I don't know anything else. I got to know of a few things that you are also aware of only after Xavier landed himself in trouble. These are big things, which innocent people like us, who go to the fellowship just to know and experience Christ, cannot understand.'

'Meaning?' Rithu, who had been quietly listening to Aunty Jovana until then, was unable to control her curiosity.

'Meaning that what is important to everyone is money. Belief is just a cover. It is really sad that my Xavier also fell into that net.'

'But this was not what you said when we met the last time, Aunty. Why did you hide all of this from us?' Sandhya asked.

'I told you what I knew then. What I know today is what I shared with you. I have nothing to hide from God and man, Sandhya.'

It was then that Xavier walked in. He looked quite hassled. Without even acknowledging them, he went straight to the kitchen, opened the refrigerator and drank cold water from a bottle. 'How did it go?' Aunty Jovana asked Xavier as she got up, walked towards him and held his hand.

'How could it have gone? Relationships thrive only on money. It is now that I understand the real meaning of St. Luke's verse, "I tell you, use worldly wealth to gain friends for yourselves, so that when it is gone, you will be welcomed into eternal dwellings." I think they are ready to send me to my eternal dwelling. Do you know Jovana, when it was that Christ was pained the most? When he saw his disciples sleeping after the prayer at Gethsemane. He even lamented that they could not stay awake with him for just a few hours. Torture, Jovana, is when you see your friends sleeping peacefully when you yourself are in acute pain. I am passing through such a phase now.'

'Please don't say such things, Xavier. We have overcome much bigger hurdles. We had no one to support us then. Now, at least these children keep coming to console us. That in itself is God's love.'

It is when Aunty Jovana said those words that Xavier actually noticed that they were in the flat. He came and sat with them and apologized. Rithu made use of his affection as well as the opportunity and asked, 'Uncle, what I find most bewildering is that a lot of people we met recently spoke about bad experiences at the fellowship. Why is that? And in spite of that, why is no one leaving the fellowship?'

'I don't think the fellowship is a bad place. It literally gives shelter to so many people. There is a sense of unity there – one which offers support, care and true bonding. It has saved many a broken life. For those who come seeking support, it is still a haven. So I will never agree if someone says that it is a place where only bad things happen. But bad things also happen there. Because certain bad people also land up there. People who use the fellowship as a cover. And make use of that cover well. For some, it is a place to make money. For some, it is a place to find business partners. For some, it is a place to flaunt their wealth. For some others, it is a way to fulfil the desires of the flesh. For yet others, a place where they can hide their dark side well. Yes, there are such people there. It is when a large cross section of ordinary folk who come there become victims of these people that we hear bad things about the fellowship. The biggest problem with the fellowship is that it has no doors to the outside – no exit. Even a thief secures himself by leaving one door open to escape. The fact remains that people who enter the fellowship in times of sorrow, misery and loneliness cannot – or do not even want to – think of an exit. They realize the situation they are in only many, many years later. It is then that they will feel the absence of that door. The other important thing is that people who join the fellowship, very often, don't have another place to go to. The only option they have is to keep everything under wraps and live out the rest of their lives without revealing anything to anyone. I won't hesitate to admit that Jovana and I are such people, who are trapped. As the saying goes, use worldly, immoral wealth to gain friends for yourselves, so that when it is gone, you will be welcomed into eternal dwellings.'

'Can you tell us about this worldly, immoral wealth? Not to make it, but to stay away from it.'

'I have always felt that young people like you are genuinely good and impartial in comparison to us elders. It is the older people who are greedy for money who are bad. They are the people who are responsible for every problem in society. They are the people who destroy nature. They are the people who destroy our mountains. They are the people who flame religious fanaticism. You are innocent. You came to the fellowship only in search of Christ. You might have gotten jobs through the fellowship. You might have earned money. But you are not as bad as we are. Ragesh, you came here a few days ago in search of a vehicle. What you need to search for is not that vehicle. You should track where Midhun's organs went. Do you know the price of a human body in today's market? A heart costs two crores. Lungs, one crore. Liver, eighty lakhs. Eyes, ten lakhs.

Kidney, eight lakhs. Pancreas, skull, bones, skin … the list goes on. Will anyone let go of such a precious thing if they get it for free? Especially people who trade organs?

'Who is that?' Sandhya was petrified.

'You and I know who that is. Why, then, should I say the names?'

57

They inspected the list of people who had shared Midhun's body again that day. It was all there in a newspaper clipping that Sandhya had filed away.

Eyes to Manisha from Bihar. Liver to Harinder Singh from Punjab. Pancreas to Sukhdev from Patna. Lungs to Abdul Aziz from Kashmir. Kidneys to Ananthakumar Rao from Karnataka. Heart to Sundar Ramaswamy, a leading businessman from Chennai. Midhun, who was declared brain-dead, was now living through these six people.

'Will it be possible to know more about these people if you search for and manage to find their hospital files?' they asked Jane.

'Don't even think about it, Rithu. Those will be top secret files. None of us will be allowed anywhere near them. Not only that, they were all in different hospitals. You can get more information about them only from there. The only patient who was in the same hospital as Midhun was the recipient of the kidneys. I remember reading in last month's issue of our *Spandanam* spiritual magazine, that he had joined the fellowship.'

'So is there a way forward, Jane?'

'There is. Manish Pandey, a junior reporter wrote the article. He had come to the hospital later to do a follow-up story. I remember seeing him then. I remember him because he looks like a Bollywood actor whom I like very much. I had even asked him if he was that actor!'

That was enough for them. Ragesh managed to get the reporter's number from the newspaper office and called him. He was busy covering a minister's press conference. He did not respond favourably to their request. He stated clearly that he was not interested in chasing an old story. However, Ragesh did not let go. He managed to hook Manish by saying that he had new, interesting information. Finally, after three days, Manish said that he could meet between five and six in the evening and hung up.

In the evening, when he called again, Manish agreed to come over to the Pizza Hut in Connaught Place. In spite of Rithu's anxiety, Ragesh sped on his bike to meet the reporter. He did call her before leaving, though, and asked her to come over there after office hours.

'Yes, I had covered that news. I did make an attempt to do a follow-up story. But realizing that nobody was interested, I dumped the idea. When you called, I thought it was to give me an update. I guess you know that we reporters only gather news – we don't share it.'

What Jane had said was true. He did look like a Bollywood actor. Not only that, he also tried to speak like him. 'This is not just for news, the person who died was a very close friend of mine. Which is why I am so involved,' said Ragesh, making things very clear. At that point, Rithu also joined them. On seeing Rithu, Manish's reluctance turned into involvement.

'Look my friend, there are so many such deaths and organ donations that happen in the city. These things are not news any more. What attracted me to this story was the fact that the recipient of the cornea, Manisha, was from a very poor family. She got the cornea as well as the subsequent treatment totally free of cost. It was big news in the city newspapers. At a time when organ donation is big business, I wanted to find out how this had happened. For that, I checked the boy's – what was his name?'

'Midhun.'

'Yes, yes, Midhun. I checked the background of all the people who had accepted his organs. Only the girl I did the story on – Manisha – was from a poor family. All the others were rich one way or another. There is no information on how much they were charged for each organ. My belief is that they would have paid four times the cost in the black market. The people who gave the cornea gratis to Manisha are very clever. That became news. That was celebrated. And behind that, the money that was collected from the other donors vanished. I had called and checked with that boy's family – they did not get any part of the money. What they got was a small token from some Trinity Foundation. Just peanuts. The information I gathered was that the recipient of the heart, Sundar Ramaswamy, a Tamil businessman, paid three crores. My effort was to find out where that money had gone.

But even my desk is not interested in such news. They are satisfied with a bit of politics every day for dinner. Then why should I care? I left that story. Do you have anything new to give me?'

'No,' Ragesh shook his head. 'Let's part then. I have other things to do.' Manish Pandey got up. They too had no option but to get up.

58

The next day, Rithu received a call from Pretty in Pune. 'You met Manish yesterday, didn't you?' And after that, unfolded a long list of complaints. 'Rithu, wasn't it me who encouraged you to start this investigation? Wasn't it me who introduced you to Jane? Why didn't you even call to tell me how far you had reached? I even came to know about Brother Aruldas's death through someone else. Am I such a stranger to all of you now? Why did I become the person who had to be left out of everything and with whom secrets could not be shared? You should at least tell me that,' Pretty went on and on.

'No, no. Don't say all that and upset me. It is definitely the encouragement that you gave me when I was in Pune that made me rise above my fear. And it was that which helped me get Ragesh and Sandhya on board. But our investigation has not really reached anywhere. We just have a bunch of clues and pointers. I thought I'd call you after we had a clearer idea. And in the midst of all this, Brother Aruldas died. That really scared us, Pretty. He had many things to tell us and he had agreed to talk to us. But before that…'

'Though you did not tell me, I more or less knew what was happening. If not, I would not have known so soon of your meeting with Manish. Do understand that there are eyes following you.'

'Who's this informer, Pretty? Is it Jane? Or someone else?'

'You might think it is Jane, but it is not. I just called her to confirm. It was Pastor Shanu who told me this. You must meet Pastor Shanu as discreetly as possible. He also wants to speak to you about something.'

'Really? We had met Pastor Shanu so many times in between. But he never expressed a desire to talk to or meet us.'

'Some people are like that, Rithu. In fact, most people are like that. They wait for the best opportunity to come along.'

'Okay. Should I call him or will he call me?'

'The pastor will call when the time is right. Please take calls from unknown numbers. He might not call you from his personal number.'

They had to wait for two more weeks for the call to come. In the meantime, Ragesh got a letter of termination from his office. He was happy to sign and receive the letter as though it was something that he had been waiting for. This avoided the long explanations and formalities that accompanied putting in one's papers. However, to the utter shock of her colleagues, Rithu also got a letter of termination the next day. Until then, she had the distinction of being the best programmer. No one could understand why, in spite of that, it was her name that featured first in the list of people the company was letting go in the guise of downsizing. Though the totally unexpected notice shocked Rithu, it did not upset her. She was just disappointed that she did not have the opportunity to walk out before she was asked to leave. It was when Sandhya too received a letter of termination three days later that they were really shocked. Until then, they had not realized that this was all part of a larger conspiracy. They knew for certain now that it was not sheer coincidence that three friends, working in three different companies, were terminated from service at the same time. Sandhya's reaction was very different from that of Ragesh and Rithu. She wept. In front of the manager. In front of HR. But both placed the onus of this decision on others and stated that they were helpless. Even Sandhya's plea to let her keep her job until her daughter got out of school that year, fell on deaf ears.

Ragesh and Rithu met in Sandhya's flat that evening. Sandhya's Uncle Carlos was there. He happened to be passing through Delhi on one of his new journeys and he had dropped in just like that. To her question, 'Do you remember me?' not only did he answer, 'Rithu', he even told her the exact date on which they had travelled together on his bike. They saluted the memory of this eighty-three-year-old man. Until the two of them walked in, Uncle Carlos had been under the impression that the sorrow on Sandhya's face was because of her divorce. When he understood why she was really upset, he consoled her saying, 'Is that all? I too have a few contacts in this country. Finding a job in this city is no big deal.' He then made a few calls. 'I will do one round and be back here in a week. By then Sandhya will have a new job,' he said, before departing on his bike.

After Uncle Carlos left, Rithu laughed. The others looked at her askance. 'If we were still believers who were part of the fellowship, we would have perceived Uncle Carlos's arrival as something mystical. God's intervention. The arrival of God's messenger. All nonsense. And now? He's just a biker who is trying to get his favourite girl a job, using his small circle of friends. There is nothing miraculous about it. It is not the experience – it is the mind that interprets the experience that slaps the label of divinity on it.'

'Rithu, are we not part of the fellowship any more?' Sandhya asked doubtfully.

'Are we? In our minds, have we not travelled too far out? Will we ever return to that island?'

59

Kurian Sir and Mamma Lally were happy when they were told about the loss of the job. The reason was simple. 'At least until you get your next job, you will come and stay at home.' However, it was not to tell them about the lost job that Rithu had actually called. It was to tell Kurian Sir that she had received his book, *The Spiritual Alvares*. It was not a great book in terms of production. But in terms of fulfilling Kurian Sir's life, it was more than enough. A critical look convinced Rithu that Kurian Sir had done his research well. Which is why she decided to present a copy each to Rithu and Ragesh. Armed with two books and a shopping bag, it was as she was stepping out that a call from an unknown number landed on her phone. It was Pastor Shanu.

'I will be leaving for Bilaspur this evening. I will be there for a week. If you come there, we can talk about a few things in detail.'

'So far?' Rithu said.

'I would have preferred it to be even further. This is a mission I am undertaking on my own. None of the brothers are travelling with me. I see this as the perfect opportunity to speak without fear. Call me on this number once you reach there.' Pastor Shanu hung up.

'How can we go to Bilaspur? This is crazy. If he has something to tell us, why can't he do that here?' an angry Rithu asked Ragesh over the phone.

'It's not like that, Rithu. We should go where the pastor wants us to. There are two things here. First, we need to give him the privacy he seeks. And second, he needs to feel that we are willing to trust him and do as he says. So whichever corner of the world he asks me to go, I will,' Ragesh interpreted it in his own way.

'You'll go alone? Do you think you will be allowed to go alone again? I have not yet recovered from the shock of Brother Aruldas's death.'

'I am not scared, Rithu. If someone has targeted you, he will get you – no matter where you are, no matter how careful you are. The best way to conquer fear is to have no fear. Going alone to Bilaspur is not a problem for me.'

'Until we leave this city, there is no way you are going anywhere alone. I am stepping out now. You check if you can get two tickets online.'

Tickets were not available. And yet, they got on the next train to Bilaspur. It was after reaching there and calling the pastor that they realized he was in a village that was another hundred and forty kilometres away. They boarded a bus and reached the village in the evening.

'Instead of speaking to you in Delhi about something that happened in Delhi, if I made you travel all the way here to have a conversation, I'm sure you will understand how scared I am of certain people,' Pastor Shanu said apologetically. 'I know certain things regarding Midhun's death. But I was in two minds about sharing them with you. I even prayed for hours to get an answer to this. And when the answer finally came, it was in the affirmative.'

Pastor Shanu stepped out with Ragesh and Rithu, and they walked a while before sitting on a bench near a lake.

'I was aware that organ trading was happening in Dr John Samuel's hospital. But I came to know of the relationship between the hospital, our fellowship and the Trinity Foundation very late. It was Brother Aruldas who told me about that. He was also an important middleman like Xavier. But the difference between them was that one person was doing it for money and the other because of his belief.'

'I don't understand, Pastor,' said Rithu.

'I'll tell you. Do you know what the contract was with the recipient of Midhun's kidney, Ananthakumar Rao? The kidney and the treatment were free of cost. In lieu of which he had to become a believer, join the fellowship, become another living testimony of the fellowship for life and retain his current name in spite of the change in faith.'

'We did not get the last bit,' Ragesh interjected.

'Why do you think I still continue to be Pastor Shanu instead of being Pastor John or Pastor Peter or Pastor Joshua? Giving Christian names to people who become believers is an old Pentecostal tradition. But fellowships like ours prefer to retain non-Christian names. You might not understand the marketing value of that. The testimony of a Brother Shanu or a Brother Ananthakumar Rao or a Brother Mustafa will attract four times the number of people than a Brother John. That's the reason – and it's the same reason why Ragesh is still Ragesh and Sandhya is still Sandhya. The Trinity Foundation is a cover for all this. It's a joint business run by Advocate Ram Manohar Varma, Dr John Samuel and Pastor Sam Philip. I guess this is something you already know. But what will shock you is the fact that there is a secret fourth partner.'

'Fourth partner?'

'A silent partner. Someone you will never be able to guess: Jesus Christ.'

'Jesus Christ? How blasphemous, Pastor!'

'They are proving that it is not blasphemous. They believe that, in the business they are running centred around the hospital, they have a fourth partner in Jesus Christ. They divide all the profit that they get into four. The fourth part goes to the poor in the name of Christ. That's what the Trinity Foundation does.'

'How can Christ...? Please Pastor, you are driving us insane.'

'People who preach that Christ will give you whatever you ask for will have no qualms in making Christ a business partner.'

'We don't believe this,' Ragesh said.

'You have the right to disbelieve. And I have the freedom to say that the lesson I learnt from life is right.'

'But Pastor, you are still…'

'Yes. Some holes are like that. Once you fall into them, there is no getting out. I am sure you understand. You are young. If you can escape, please do. Just hold on tight to Christ. Forget everything else.'

60

Three people were saying goodbye to the city of Delhi on the same day. One was on a train to Goa and the other was on a train to Chennai. The third, on a bus to Kasol. Jane had come to Sandhya's flat to see them off. It was what she said then that stayed in their minds as they started their respective journeys.

'Two days before Midhun died, I had a very strange experience at the hospital. There was a file without the name and the address of the patient on Dr Samuel's table. I looked at it out of curiosity. It was the summary of a detailed examination of a patient. ECG and treadmill tests had been done. The blood report from the lab was there. An X-ray had also been taken. But the name of the person was not there. Who was that? Why were the diagnostic tests carried out? Nothing was clear. We can only guess based on what we know. At this time, I am not even sharing that hunch. That too, I leave for you to investigate.'

Throughout the journey, Rithu kept thinking of what Jane had said to them. Somewhere in between, a man in white came, sat next to her and gifted her a Bible with a black cover. She accepted it with a half-smile and placed it in her bag. When he started to say something, she gestured with her hand that she was not interested in a conversation. Then she stretched out on the seat and slept.

In the morning, when she alighted at Madgaon, the city seemed busier than usual. It was only later that Rithu realized that Goa was going through the 'Exposition', when the mortal remains of St. Francis Xavier are kept for public viewing, something which happens only once in ten years. The city was crowded with believers who had come in hordes to the Basilica of Bom Jesus. People who came for the magic that they believed would happen after they had a glimpse of the saint. Rithu recalled standing in a long queue somewhere to see St. Francis when she was a child. But she had no recollection of what she saw. Yet, she did not feel like going to the Exposition. Instead, she went straight to the grave of Pastor Alvares, laid to rest in one corner of the municipal cemetery of the Sé Cathedral. With no one to tend to it, the grave was covered in grass and weeds.

Rithu put her shoulder bag down and cleaned his resting place. She then she lit a candle for him, which she managed to get from the front yard of the church. She felt that the candle emanated more light than usual. Rithu experienced an inexplicable energy flowing through her. Rejuvenated, she walked back home. She had a Bible with a black cover in her bag. That was all she needed for self-confidence.